To Live Out Loud

A Novel

PAULETTE MAHURIN

ISBN: 978-0-9888468-9-0

Published by Early Girl Enterprises, LLC

Printed in the United States of America

For my cousins

Acknowledgment

Thank you, Margaret Dodd, for your expertise editing and feedback. This book would not have moved forward without you. And to Dr. Lorna Lee, the brilliant author and my beta reader, you gave this story the polish it needed for the final touches. I'm forever grateful for your assistance. To Terry, my husband and rock, you were there through it all, reading, editing, cooking my meals, and being incredibly supportive. Everything I do is possible because of your love.

To those who have endured intolerance and adversity because of your religious beliefs, your sexual preference, or the color of your skin, you have inspired and deeply moved me to write, to remember you.

Lastly, to all the Zolas of the world a heartfelt thank you for your heroic endeavors. More innocent victims would be in graves were it not for your selfless kindness.

To Live Out Loud

If you ask me what I came into this life to do, I will tell you:
I came to live out loud.

Émile Zola

To Live Out Loud

Foreword

Although this story is a historical fiction, much of what you will read is documented historical fact. Many of the scenes, some of the content in the narrative, and sections of the dialogue have been taken from historical references. For example, Lucie Dreyfus's letter to the court came from the transcript of Émile Zola's libel trial. The court scenes and accompanying dialogue came from the same source. Émile Zola's communications were taken from articles and letters he wrote in the Paris newspaper, *L'Aurore*. When finding accurate and complete data proved difficult, scenes were created. Such was the case with Émile Zola's death. The protagonist, Charles Mandonette, is a fictionalized character—modeled from his friendship with Henry Vizetelly and his son, Ernest Alfred Vizetelly. In the book, "Émile Zola Novelist and Reformer: An Account of his Life Work," Ernest Alfred Vizetelly transcribes his father's journal and writes about his memories of events in Zola's life. Henry Vizetelly was a close friend and publisher for Émile Zola. His son, Ernest, witnessed many of the scenes described in this book. Fact was mingled with fiction to create a coherent, fluid narrative that remained true to this compelling moment in time and these people who were a part of it.

To Live Out Loud

Prologue

On a cold January morning in 1895, Alfred Dreyfus was paraded out into the courtyard of the École Militaire on the Champ de Mars. A young Jewish artillery officer, husband, and father, he had been convicted of treason a few days earlier in a hasty court-martial. "I am innocent," he proclaimed over and over. In accordance with French military custom, he was ceremoniously degraded in public by having rank insignia, buttons, and braid cut from his uniform, and his dress sword broken. The crowd cheered as he was made to march around the grounds in his tattered uniform with his head bowed.

Continuing to repeat, "I am innocent," sweat dripped from his body.

"Judas!" roared an obese man with a beard.

"Traitor!" screamed others. "Dirty Jews. Get rid of all of them! You have ruined France!"

Dreyfus cried, "I am innocent. I love France."

With each plea, the crowd's din grew louder. "Lock the Jew up!"

Hidden discretely in a far back corner, a thin woman wearing black wept for her husband, whom she knew had been falsely accused. The shock was fresh; the reality had not yet taken hold. "This can't be happening," she sobbed. "It can't be real."

Also present was a dignified heavily bearded man wearing glasses, finely dressed in a cape and beret. Standing silently, he shook his head at the disgraceful sight unfolding before him. The man next to him was making a drawing of the scene for the cover of *Le Petit Journal, Supplement Illustre*. The bearded man questioned him. "Why would someone, who fought so hard to rise to the heights he has, risk it?"

"Good question, Émile," responded the artist.

Émile Zola nodded. "Yes," he replied, "a question I am curious about."

I am an artist. The artist is nothing without the gift, but the gift is nothing without the work.

Émile Zola

Chapter One

The first time I laid eyes on Émile Zola it was 1843. He was no taller than my knee, a boy only three years old. A loquacious child tirelessly questioning all his eyes took in he was his father's joy. One friend of his father would laugh that he was destined to use his voice for great things. This innocent boy playing with his papers could never know that his curiosity would lead him into the muck of one of the most shameful episodes of French history.

I was fortunate that his gifted father, François, from a friendly Venetian family, hired me at his newly formed company in Aix-en-Provence. As a collective group of engineers, we worked together on a plan designed by Zola to create a dam and canal to supply fresh water to the city. That François and I would become close friends became apparent in my first interview.

"Mr. Charles Mandonette," he said, glancing at the page before him, hand printed in my neatest manner, "you have impressive work experience. I see you went to Aix Marseille University and are also an engineer, like me." He looked up to make eye contact and added, "Although you are a few years younger." He laughed, referring to my age of twenty-two. He seemed to be in his mid-thirties.

The warmth he radiated gave me comfort. "Yes, Mr. Zola, this is one of the reasons I wish to work with you. I want to continue to learn and grow." My own parents were deceased, and having no siblings, something about him spoke to my longing to belong, to find the family taken from me by yellow fever. While on vacation I was left inside for a nap when the mosquitos found my parents outside. After they died, I was sent to an orphanage. All I knew of family was from the nuns who took care of me and educated me through school until I went to university. Attending at an age younger than most, it was there that I became friends with other engineering students.

"That's a fine attitude, Charles. And what exactly were your engineering duties at your former place of employment?" he asked.

I explained the project I had worked on, which was brought to a successful completion, leaving me available and in need of a new job. His smile suggested that I would not be spending the last of my savings on my next month's rent. He went on to hire me with a celebratory meal at his home that night. It was there I met his French wife, Émilie, and son, Émile.

Émile pointed a finger at me as he stuffed a piece of baguette into his mouth. Before he could say a word, his father interrupted with, "Do not speak with food in your mouth, my son."

Still pointing, he finished what he was chewing and asked, "Who are you?"

"I am Charles Mandonette. And who might you be?"

Giggling, he replied, "I'm Émile." He looked at the loaf of bread then at his parents. Upon his father's nod he said, "Here," as he passed the plate to me. "It's very good."

We laughed at the endearing manner of this precocious child. The laughter ended four years later, when my friend and mentor, François Zola, died from pneumonia before the water project was completed. His death left his wife to struggle with an increasingly difficult financial situation. A meager pension barely sustained them. Despite this, young seven-year-old Émile enjoyed his boyhood and schooling in Aix, where he became close friends with Paul Cézanne. The two boys spent hours debating topics important to them. In these dialectics, Émile developed a trait of defending against injustices. This attribute would stay with him for the rest of his life serving him years later when he would write an exposé in the press against powerful resistance.

As for me, I found other work, and maintained a close friendship with Mrs. Zola and Émile. Whether from the premature death of his father or the need for a man in his life, Émile took to me as a confidant. Having never married, I valued this substitute father-son relationship, and was grateful it continued when in 1858 he moved with his mother to Paris. There he went on with his education but never succeeded in passing his baccalauréate examination. For a few years after leaving school he struggled to make ends meet, and were it not for my supplementing the small earnings he acquired from odd jobs, he would have been destitute. On many weekends, I traveled from Aix to Paris to spend time with him.

"Should I pursue my dream to write?" he asked.

"To what end? And by what means?" I questioned.

"For love. And voice. I'm driven to communicate, to write." He sighed. "Who makes a living writing? Perhaps I should forsake my passion."

His furrowed brow and inward gaze showed his discouragement, to which I responded, "If you follow your passion, using prudence and wisdom and an ethical conscience, with your gift you might find luck."

"Luck says it, doesn't it? But I've not been lucky thus far in life. My father. My education. Mother's struggle."

"The past doesn't have to dictate the future. Trust your intuition to guide you where you need to go."

Shortly after, in 1862, as I sat in a Parisian café with him and Cézanne, he announced, "I've been given a position with the Hachette publishing firm. And I am going to become a naturalized citizen of France," referring to the French nationality law that requires children born in France of foreign parents to request citizenship at adulthood.

§ § § §

The years following were good to Zola. He stayed at Hachette for four years learning the business and the promotional side of publishing, and met several esteemed writers. Not long after that, he made decent money as a freelance journalist. Around that time I partially retired and moved to Paris.

"I've met a woman, Alexandrine," he glowed, "whom I plan to marry."

"At twenty-six, you've acquired the wisdom and patience needed to live with another," I said, patting him on the back.

That relationship was childless. After the death of his ailing mother who lived with them, he fell in love with a young seamstress, Jeanne Rozerot, with whom he had two children. He remained married and close friends with his wife, who painfully understood and accepted his desire for offspring. Zola maintained two households: his primary home was with Alexandrine, but he spent as much time as he could with Jeanne and the children. His writing during that time showed a sunnier disposition, which he attributed to his domestic happiness.

As he aged and continued to write, he grew into an accomplished, respected journalist. He was ripe for the dramatic intervention he would take on behalf of Alfred Dreyfus.

I am little concerned with beauty or perfection. I don't care for the great centuries. All I care about is life, struggle, and intensity.

Émile Zola

Chapter Two

It was a clear cold day in Paris on January 13, 1895 when *Le Petit Journal, Supplement Illustre,* hit the streets. On the cover was a drawing of the École Militaire courtyard with a young Jewish artillery officer in a plain uniform devoid of medals and ribbons. His dress sword was being broken across the knee of a senior officer as the dejected man stood guarded by a number of military men. Zola had told me it was one of the worst public scenes of degradation he'd ever witnessed. The gawking crowd went wild, screaming "Jew! Traitor!" as Dreyfus professed his innocence.

I purchased the newspaper and walked past cafés with braziers outside keeping their jovial patrons warm. Their laughter rang in my head as I thought of Dreyfus serving a life sentence on Devil's Island in French Guiana. I couldn't clear my mind of what Zola had told me—that Dreyfus had gone to the prestigious war college, graduated with honorable mention, and was designated as a trainee in the French Army's General Staff Headquarters. *Why would he risk so much?* It didn't make sense to me. Zola had concurred.

I arrived at the bistro where I was to meet Émile and noticed the article on the table. "Ah, you too," I said.

"The whole of Paris… France… most likely will be talking about this today," he replied.

"And we shan't be an exception," I laughed.

"I think not," Zola smiled. "I ordered a carafe of red wine." He moved an empty glass over to me. "Help yourself."

I drank while he held up the drawing.

"That day was like something out of medieval Europe; the Inquisition comes to mind. That poor man kept bellowing his innocence with such conviction that it was hard to disbelieve him. And I am not so sure that I accept the veracity of the accusations against him. From my perspective, it simply doesn't add up."

"Yes, I have the same sense. Why would he risk everything he'd achieved? No small feat for a Jewish man in France."

"Excellent point, Charles. Of all things, he yelled out, 'Long live France, and long live the army' with immense certitude." Zola finished his glass of wine and poured another. "The oddest thing he said, 'I remain worthy of serving the army,' is hardly something a guilty traitor would be screaming after being found out. It violates my sense of logic."

"I suppose we'll never know the truth." I looked into his pensive eyes, and commented, "You look as though you want to say something."

"If this is some kind of conspiracy, France's identity as a republic founded on equal rights for all will come into question for castigating a man of Jewish faith. If, and it's a big if," he sucked in a slow breath, "Catholic France is involved, it threatens to divide the nation."

Little did he know that nearly two years later, in November 1896, news would leak to the press of a cover-up and Dreyfus's probable innocence. It would engender a national fiery debate on France's position regarding equal rights versus anti-Semitism that would forever alter Zola's life.

Sin ought to be something exquisite, my dear boy.

Émile Zola

Chapter Three

On that frigid January day back in 1895 when Alfred Dreyfus was humiliated, what was seen publicly—on the Champ de Mars in the shadow of the Eiffel Tower, the monument of changing times—had started a year earlier. French Army's Intelligence Service was alerted that a spy in a high position was passing data on to the Germans. The assumption: the hostile operative was most likely on the General Staff and that Dreyfus was the spy.

Later, after the Dreyfus court-martial, the new chief of military intelligence, Lt. Colonel Georges Picquart, found evidence that the real traitor was Major Ferdinand Esterhazy. When he reported this to his seniors, he was transferred to the southern desert of Tunisia to silence him. Esterhazy, the real culprit, was tried in a sham military court. After two days he was unanimously acquitted.

Now, almost two years after Dreyfus had been imprisoned in a solitary, cold prison cell, word of the cover-up began to spread, eventually leaking to the press. And to Zola.

"I can feel the wave of hatred rolling over France as we speak, Charles," Zola said, shaking his head disapprovingly.

"We suspected as much early on. But what if this is a ploy as well, a further cover-up?"

"Anything is possible with military politics," he replied. "Heaven forbid a mistake is exposed in the war machine."

"Yes, hubris does thrive there," I laughed.

Zola gave me a look.

"I know this is not a laughing matter."

He nodded.

"I feel for the poor wife and children," I said.

"I feel for Dreyfus," he said as he exhaled. "It never added up in the first place. Probably being the only Jew on the General Staff, he was the most likely target once the leak of documents to the German Embassy was discovered."

"What now?"

"Everything has been suppressed." His words spit out in snake-like hisses as he continued, "No one is going to touch it. The military machine has denied any wrongdoing. I don't know what now. When hatred is involved, it burns flames that are near impossible to extinguish."

That night I had trouble sleeping. Tossing and turning, I was unable to stop thinking of Zola's last comment about hatred. I imagined all sorts of scenarios, knowing that anything resembling reality would not have a good ending against the might and power of the military. If Dreyfus was innocent, military hubris and concealment would most likely still win out. Too bad this wasn't ancient Greece, when hubris was a high crime. Perhaps that would be a deterrent. How fragile the ethics of civilized conduct are when involved in self-preservation. My final thought was, God help us all.

§ § § §

As Dreyfus was rotting away on Devil's Island, the wheels of justice were turning very slowly. Vindication was, as yet, far off on the foggy horizon. The next week, when Zola and I shared another bottle of wine, I inquired, "Was he the accidental victim of a well-planned plot, and if so, what connected him with the German Embassy?"

"Good question, Charles." He sipped his wine.

"Is the assumption that he was targeted because he's Jewish?" I asked.

"Probably. But he also had family in Mulhouse."

"Mulhouse?"

"It's still under German occupancy."

"Yes, of course. How did you learn that he had family there?"

"Curiosity, my friend, curiosity."

"And," I laughed, "resources."

"The interesting thing is," he continued, referring to the most recent leaked data, "that the French Army Intelligence had an agent in the German Embassy—a cleaning woman." He filled his glass again.

"And?"

"At night she emptied the wastebaskets of a high-ranking German military attaché. She brought the trash to her supervisors, and on one occasion they found torn-up pieces of a bordereau. When the pieces were assembled, it was discovered that someone from our side was offering to sell military secrets."

Shaking my head, I replied, "And they targeted Dreyfus for this because he's a Jew and has family living in a German section of France? How did that ever hold up?"

"That's not all." He scratched his chin. "The secrets to be sold ostensibly pointed to an artillery officer. With Dreyfus's connection to Mulhouse…"

Interrupting him, I said, "The Intelligence Service must have loved that," alluding to the prejudice it had against Jews entering into high ranks in the military.

"Right you are. What apparently cinched the deal was a handwriting expert who compared the memorandum with Dreyfus's handwriting. Under pressure he must have come up with some bogus proof. I don't remember everything I read but it smelled fishy to me."

"So then what was leaked to the press to question whether Dreyfus had been falsely accused?

"I was wondering when you'd ask me that," he smiled.

"Well?"

"Apparently evidence came to light from an investigation ordered by the head of Intelligence."

"Picquart?"

"Yes, and it identified someone else."

"Who?"

"That's where the leaked data stops."

"Talk about suspense!" I was distracted by a group of men sitting at a nearby table, their voices raised in slurs at each other.

"The last interesting piece of information," Zola leaned in across the table so I'd hear him over the raucous activity, "is that Picquart was transferred to a position in Africa."

"Shame! He's one of the decent leaders…so popular."

"Exactly!"

"Are you planning on pursuing an article on this?"

"No."

"Then this is only to satisfy your desire to know what's going on?"

"For now, let's just say that's most likely the case. The inquisitive bug has caught me." He looked around to be sure no one was paying attention to us or could hear him when in a strained murmur he said, "Any writer or journalist to touch this risks prosecution for libel."

I have but one passion: to enlighten those who have been kept in the dark, in the name of humanity, which has suffered so much and is entitled to happiness.

Émile Zola

Chapter Four

If anti-Semitism didn't incite the proceedings leading to Dreyfus's imprisonment, it certainly fueled it. How could the army possibly vindicate a Jew, even when the evidence surfaced that the facts were wrong, misconstrued, or altered in the first place? To view the injustice without a reminder of France's history and identification as a Catholic nation would be to blindly look at hatred with the justification of innocence. To understand this is to understand the huge popularity of a book published in the 1880s by Edouard Drumont, *Jewish France,* which focused on the influx of Jewish immigrants from Germany and Eastern Europe. Drumont wrote that Jews brought with them an ideology foreign to Christianity, convincing readers that France's real debacle was the decline of Christian faith. He made a strong case for the corrupt influence that the modern art and traditions of the Jewish people had on France.

The popularity of Drumont's book was praised in the Catholic newspaper *La Croix,* which ignited the flame of anti-Semitism. Further ammunition was the fact that many French believed that Germany was the true religious home of the Jews because of the 1869 North German Confederation, a law that abolished former restrictions imposed on religious worship. Since Jews were religiously bound to Germany, the argument that they were politically allied with the Germans was an easy one for the French to make. I didn't believe it, but it was easy for me to see how the stage had been set for my fellow countrymen to believe that a Jewish man would use his high rank in the French military against his country.

That prejudice, in combination with the humiliation the army would face were Dreyfus found innocent, was reason enough to sweep the whole affair, facts and all, under the carpet. To the accusers, Dreyfus was the most hated man in France. They believed he deserved to be ripped from his wife and children and sent to deteriorate on a forsaken island in the Atlantic. That he was not even allowed out of his cell to see the ocean that surrounded him was of no concern to his enemies. Therefore it was no wonder that the unraveling of the Dreyfus injustice moved along at a snail's pace, preoccupying the minds of those involved, like my dear friend Zola and me.

§ § § §

Alfred Dreyfus's father, Raphael, was a self-made prosperous man in the textile business. Speaking only Yiddish and German, he had moved with his wife and nine children from Germany to Alsace-Lorraine in France. At the end of the Franco-Prussian War when Alsace was annexed by Germany, he moved with his family to Paris. Many of his relatives remained in Alsace. As Alfred and his siblings grew, they would visit them. It was this geographical displacement by the war that motivated Alfred to decide on a career in the military. His brother, Mathieu, remained in the family's textile business and supported Alfred's family while Alfred was imprisoned. The well-to-do Mathieu was friends with Auguste Scheurer-Kestner, Vice President of the French Senate. Also a friend with Scheurer-Kestner was Zola.

§ § § §

On a lazy, humid Saturday afternoon, when I didn't have plans with Zola or other friends I'd connected with since moving to Paris, I decided to go to the library. Motivated by Zola's disturbed countenance when last we spoke, I wanted to better understand the roots of the hatred levied at Dreyfus. As I made my way down the Champs-Elysées past its gardens and trees, with the Arc de Triomphe in sight, I came to the Avenue du Trocadero—an uncanny coincidence. I had heard that it was the street where Dreyfus lived with his wife Lucie and their two young children, Pierre and Jeanne. A heaviness set into my chest as I imagined them fatherless.

Although I was well taken care of by the nuns who raised me, I knew the feeling—that empty place in a child's heart, the yearning for one's parents. I have missed them all my life. It was this craving in my soul, to be where I belong and with whom I am loved, that drove me to know more about the circumstances surrounding the Dreyfus family.

I started my search through the stacks of books and came across an abundance of material on French history, but what caught my attention was a book on the Franco-Prussian War. Letting my instincts guide me, I picked it up and began reading. I had found what I wanted.

In the early 1870s, when France was occupied by foreign troops and Adolphe Thiers came into power, there was much bloodshed with two provinces annexed to Germany. Afterwards, national pride and vengeance preoccupied the French people. It was at this time that an influx of Jewish immigrants poured into France. France was a devoutly Christian country and suspicious of this invasion of non-believers. Anti-

Semitism spread easily throughout the country. Like any group, the French people were a family—sharing traditions, history, and a common faith. Now this family was being threatened. I understand the fear that comes when an enemy, seen or unseen, jeopardizes one's family. The irony was that the Dreyfus family endured the same fear; only now the enemy was the French. Nausea rose in my belly as I reflected back on the spilled blood, ruined and lost lives caused from the anger that seeded hatred.

To Live Out Loud

Respectable people…What bastards!

Émile Zola

Chapter Five

Zola had had a meal with Auguste Scheurer-Kestner and wanted to talk with me. At ten in the morning he appeared at my door. His voice quivered as he said, "I'm disgusted. I need my friend."

"Come in. Sit," I motioned to a chair in my kitchen. "I'll put some hot water on. You look as though you haven't slept."

"Then my looks don't belie me."

I poured tea into a cup and handed it to him.

"Thank you," he said. "I met with Scheurer-Kestner."

"Bad news?"

"Yes! It piles on and reaches a point where it's just too much. I can understand the cover-up, that's what politicians do." Clutching the cup in his hand, "It's the nature of the beast to those in power, but to have the facts point to his innocence and be completely suppressed? To continue to perpetuate the horrific lies when…"

"You're overly annoyed," I interrupted. "Something new?"

"Auguste is also friends with Dreyfus's brother. They've been communicating."

"Oh, I see. And?"

"Mathieu, Dreyfus's brother, is working tirelessly to free him. He's gathering evidence that has leaked…"

"From Scheurer-Kestner?"

"Yes," he sneered.

The smugness in Zola's tone perplexed me. "Why are you smirking at that? A government official talking to a civilian about military affairs won't be looked at kindly."

"The leaks are happening from too many places to lay blame on any one individual. Plus, Mathieu has a vested interest to keep confidential his sources," said Zola.

"Surely others know he's friends with the Vice President of the French Senate," I replied.

"Mathieu Dreyfus is a man of wealth with friends in high places. Plus many in positions of authority, not privy to military affairs, are catching wind that Alfred Dreyfus was unfairly rushed through his court-martial and that solid evidence exists as to who the real traitor is. Here's where it gets particularly entangled." He went on to tell me that Scheurer-Kestner had learned that a Major Ferdinand Esterhazy's stockbroker had seen a photograph of the bordereau published in a newspaper. "He recognized the handwriting as his client! Clearly discernable and unmistakable, it was Esterhazy who wrote the treasonous memorandum to give secrets to the Germans."

I nearly fell off my chair. "Surely, you're joking."

"I kid you not," Zola continued, "and so Scheurer-Kestner felt that if this is so loosely spoken of, then what is the harm to share a snippet or two with Dreyfus's brother, a good friend of his?"

"What now?"

"The brother will plead a case for retrial."

"Good luck with that." I sipped my drink and waited for a response. When none came, I said, "Don't you think the military will do everything in its power to obscure anything like this from being found out and validated? To them it will not matter that the stockbroker recognized the handwriting. There will be some pseudo proof to negate him." Looking into Zola's troubled eyes, I said, "Now I understand why you are so upset. It is frustrating."

The conversation lasted through the morning, switching to his telling me of the misfortune of Cézanne, who had been stricken with diabetes. He had heard about it from a mutual friend. "The illness affected his personality and relationships," Zola relayed. A sorrow overcame me as I recalled their longtime friendship, until their falling out when Zola wrote a fictionalized rendering of Cézanne and the Bohemian life of painters in his novel, *The Masterpiece*. Cézanne then withdrew into himself, spending less time with Zola. Consequently, Zola began to rely more on me.

"It is a shame you two no longer spend time together," I said.

"Yes," Zola responded. "I've often wondered about the wisdom of my approach in my writing about him."

I put my hand on his. "It's not easy to portend the regret that may come from our words."

Oh, the fools, like a lot of good little schoolboys, scared to death of anything they've been taught is wrong!

Émile Zola

Chapter Six

Mathieu Dreyfus demonstrated intelligence and wisdom in portraying the case for justice when he put the focus of his communications on correcting an error rather than on vengeance. It was important to assume the stance that the injustice was a result of human error, rather than a gross evil that had been done on purpose. He knew well that the door to his brother's vindication would stay closed with an assault on the reputation of the army. It would not work to attack its virtue.

"Mr. Dreyfus has been making waves," Zola said, referring to Alfred Dreyfus's brother.

"How so?"

"Dare you ask," he laughed. "Apparently the evidence he has unearthed is too abundant to deny. The new boys in politics are considering acting on it."

"Long live the progressives!" I cheered.

"Don't get too excited. They might not have sway with the military. Look what happened to Piquart. He apparently followed the facts and we know where it got him. He is no friend of the Jews yet he, a righteous man, defended the truth, even if it went against his own prejudice," said Zola, referring to Piquart's upbringing in Alsace and his expressed acrimony over the Jewish infiltration.

"Admirable. If only there were more like him in politics and in the military."

"Yes, but bear in mind that this is a matter larger than the question of a persecuted Jew and the army," Zola said as he pushed his pince-nez back up to the bridge of his nose, the string dangling on his cheek.

"French history, yes. I spent time in the library trying to understand the deeper issues at hand."

"Regardless of the progressive's stance gaining power, anyone who takes up the Dreyfus case risks accruing enemies. Powerful ones."

Perspiration was visible on my friend's wrinkled brow. Zola's near obsession with following the details surrounding Dreyfus's imprisonment and his brother's actions to exonerate him were clearly weighing on this man for whom justice was part of every breath. It was time to change the subject. "How is Jeanne?" I asked, referring to his mistress.

Wiping wetness from his forehead, "Keeping busy with the children," he smiled. "But then she has the youth and energy to keep up with them," he said, referring to the fact that Jeanne Rozerot was twenty-seven years younger than him. "They are growing so fast."

Relieved to see him smile, I nodded my pleasure.

"Denise is turning into a tall beauty," said Zola, referring to his daughter. "And my boy, Jacques, is gaining muscle."

I thought of these two beautiful children, attractive Jeanne, and Zola's distinguished looks, and reflected on my plain aspect. My brown hair had turned gray and my skin was pale from age; yet, in my mid-seventies, I still felt young inside. Having friends much younger than my years, including Zola's artist and writer cohorts, who never ceased to be entertaining, kept me energetic.

"The children are my joy." Zola's eyes held mine. "Thank you for understanding that there is too much commotion in the house to have our talks there. And in the other home, Alexandrine is forever inviting friends over to keep her company."

Zola was referring to the fact that we had taken to cafés for conversations, a change from regular invitations to his place for meals prepared by his wife Alexandrine. "I'm happy to accommodate you," I laughed. "I understand."

Although he never brought the subject up with me, he gave me a look that made me wonder if he questioned why I never became involved with a woman. I looked into his handsome face, his eyes glowing, and my heart knew that his friendship was love enough. I didn't miss intimacy with a woman and never fully understood why. Perhaps it was the way the nuns raised me, at a warm distance, and then again it may have been my seeing at an early age the human condition for what it was—jealousy, coveting, wanting more, and dissatisfaction with what is. Somehow blessed with a good temperament, I did not suffer from the lack of female companionship.

They dared not peer down into their own natures,
down into the feverish confusion that filled their minds
with a kind of dense, acrid mist.

Émile Zola

Chapter Seven

As the months moved on, Mathieu gained momentum in his endeavor to free his brother. The permissive left-wing politicians, fearful and reticent at first, became involved in the cause, among them the current newspaperman and future Prime Minister of France, Georges Clemenceau. None of them Jewish, they took up the cause because they wanted to see right done and end the burlesque of justice. It was clear to me that they wanted France to be true to its affirmed rules. I thanked the heavens for the growing support.

Persuasive was the mounting case against Ferdinand Esterhazy. In addition to the recognition of his handwriting on the memo that convicted Dreyfus, there was also a mountain of circumstantial evidence that cast him as a shoddy individual of dubious character. Using the lineage of the Esterhazy name, he claimed to be a count, an honor to which he was not entitled.

His commission to the French Foreign Legion was provided by an uncle's influence, which was highly irregular. It went against the custom, which was to be promoted from the ranks or to be a commissioned officer, neither of which he had attained. When it was discovered how he obtained his status in this elite corps, he was transferred to the army, employed to translate German in the French Military Intelligence Service. There he connected with players who were to be featured in the Dreyfus scandal. While never appearing at the regiment for daily work, for many years he continued to lead an extravagant life beyond his means, squandering his modest inheritance. Driven to desperation, he tried to regain money by gambling, without success. Esterhazy was two-faced. He gained assistance from the Rothschild family, prominent Jewish bankers, under false claims while winning favor with and supplying information to the editors of the anti-Semitic newspaper *La Libre Parole*. Even his physical appearance projected a character of questionable repute. Esterhazy was a man of small stature, with short legs, and hunched shoulders. He was suspicious-looking with his narrow set-eyes and prominent ears. Were he not so heinous I would have thought him a ridiculous caricature.

As the external pressure was building, so was the volcano inside Zola. Sitting before me, with cheeks puffing in an attempt to catch his breath, he said, "How can so many ignorant men be so antipathetic to speaking the truth?"

"You have answered your own question, Émile. Ignorance." My own concern arose, not just for the travesty we were discussing, but I feared that Zola would break an artery in his heart.

"This idiot," Zola said, referring to Esterhazy, "was broke! He took to gambling! He had connections linking him to the espionage."

"Yes, and the handwriting recognition." I regretted I'd let this comment slip for I knew it would fuel the fire. I softened my voice. "But then we don't know all the specifics."

"Nonsense, Charles!"

"Émile," I paused for effect, "the impact this is having on you isn't healthy."

He slammed a fist down on the table, "How can they sleep at night?" Patrons at nearby tables of the bistro we were at turned toward him.

Lowering his tone, he said, "I would like to scream at them," meaning the army in particular, "to wake up and take back their dignity." He moved his head across the table and in a whisper said, "Lying, unethical, deceitful bastards."

In an attempt to calm him, I patted his arm. In past conversations, where he had been discreet and concerned about not being heard, he was now too emotionally driven to continue safely. Attracting attention while discussing an anti-military stance in defense of Dreyfus was dangerous. If the wrong ears overheard him, the consequences were unthinkable.

Understanding my body language, he switched the topic. With the edge still in his tone, he said, "I have become aware that my writing has inspired Gustave Charpentier to begin work on a libretto for an opera." His dull eyes lightened. "It seems that my words on French naturalism are reaching wider than your ears."

"Every day, reality is making headway. Not to denigrate romanticism, but I prefer subjects that are down to earth."

"That's because you are an engineer," he smiled.

I was relieved to see him look amused. It was a mood that was not to last long.

When lovers kiss on the cheeks, it is because they are searching, feeling for one another's lips.

Émile Zola

Chapter Eight

As rumors continued to leak and the word spread, the division in France widened. Far exceeding the personal injustice of Alfred Dreyfus—his guilt or innocence—the issues took on a national perspective. The anti-Dreyfusards, as they came to be known, were against reopening the case. They saw the consideration of Dreyfus's innocence as a threat to national security. It was seen as an endeavor by the country's enemies to dishonor the army and as a global threat from international socialism and Jewry infiltration, or as a direct assault on France from Germany. Those in favor of Dreyfus's exoneration saw its suppression as a gross affront on the principle of freedom of the citizen—citizens subjugated by military rule in the name of national security. Those who were pro-Dreyfus were fighting for liberty, justice, and equality under a humane and civil France.

As the word spread and Mathieu Dreyfus continued to tirelessly campaign for his brother's retrial, Lucie Dreyfus came into public focus. Working along with her brother-in-law for the revision of the miscarriage of justice levied against her husband, she also met with Auguste Scheurer-Kestner.

Lucie Hadamard Dreyfus was born to a devout Jewish family, her father a wealthy diamond merchant and her mother a mild-mannered quiet woman who tended to her children. In 1889, only a few years before the debacle involving her husband, she and Alfred met at her parent's home. They were married the next year by the head rabbi of France in the main synagogue in Paris. Their first child, Pierre, was born in 1891. Two years later, a daughter, Jeanne, followed. A family devoted to each other, they enjoyed a peaceful, comfortable, and wealthy life.

By a stroke of uncanny circumstance, Zola ran into Auguste Scheurer-Kestner dining with Mathieu and Lucie. In a bistro the next day, he relayed to me how taken he was with her beauty—a petite woman with a charming face. "Her deep brown eyes, slightly up-turned nose, and full lips, expressed a thousand tons of sorrow." She moved him, and went straight to the place in his heart where reason is thrown to the wind.

"Be careful of getting emotionally involved," I told him.

"One cannot help it. When I looked into her eyes I wanted to weep. She tried to disguise her feelings but anyone with compassion couldn't miss her agony. She holds the pain for all of us. So does the brother. It's a sad state of affairs."

"Yes," I nodded.

"They mentioned compiling the data into a request for a retrial. And…" Zola's expression shifted inward with a troubled look.

"What?" I questioned.

"Auguste asked me to sit with them, but Lucie had to go home to tend to her children and Mathieu left with her."

"Perhaps they were uncomfortable discussing the matter with you present?"

"Yes, of course, that may well be."

"Why that look," referring to his squinting eyes.

"Auguste is concerned that the calamity will not escape the army's clutch, that it may claim it's a matter of national security and suppress any data it has. And be damned with the facts."

"The army has already shown that to be the case, hasn't it?"

"Yes."

"What about the evidence that has accumulated?" I asked.

"What about it? It was there when the original trial took place. Apparently it was withheld from Dreyfus's attorney."

When he sprang this on me, I was dumbfounded. Was I so naïve to think this whole affair couldn't possibly get any worse? "What!" I lowered my voice, "And you think it can all be suppressed?"

"History is a predictor of what will come, isn't it?" Zola looked away at something that caught his attention. After two men passed by us, he continued, "But at least now Dreyfus has some of the liberals on his side. There was another disturbing comment."

I held my breath and waited.

Zola pursed his lips, and spoke hardly above a whisper when he said, "Auguste suggested that if the attempt to gain a retrial fails, I could write something. He feels that my reputation is lofty enough that it would be published and may be another option for an inroad."

"Are you joking?"

"Afraid not."

"You know what you'd risk if you took that on?" I didn't expect an answer.

"God only knows." He pensively looked out the window. The silence between us remained.

One forges one's style on the terrible anvil of daily deadlines.

Émile Zola

Chapter Nine

True to form in his typically foolhardy though well-calculated manner, Esterhazy demanded a court-martial to clear his name. Once again he gambled, knowing the odds were in his favor since the army would support him to protect itself. The precipitous military court was held in secret. Just as Esterhazy had speculated, the military maneuvered the proceedings to both his and their mutual advantage. All the facts showing Dreyfus's innocence and Esterhazy's culpability were suppressed, resulting in a predictable acquittal for the guilty man. It was the fastest court-martial in France's history. I don't understand how men can live with themselves and sleep at night when they commit these unconscionable actions.

When the news came to the Dreyfus family, they consulted with Scheurer-Kestner. He suggested that perhaps the way to go was to have the press print the story, facts included.

Although Zola was not surprised at the audacity of the court, he was agitated by it. He appeared at my door, fit to be tied. "Where has decency gone?" he shouted, storming past me as I let him in to talk.

I knew when he cut back on his wine consumption and drank milk instead that he was developing a peptic ulcer from his preoccupation with the Dreyfus situation. Walking to my kitchen, I said, "I will make some chamomile tea. Go and sit down and relax."

"Relax," he grumbled, "not likely!"

"Émile," I said as I handed him the cup, "I'm uneasy with how you look, worn and tired, with an acid stomach, I'm assuming."

"Yes, you're right, Charles, but it seems I am about to be invited to get involved."

"Why do you say that?"

"I've been offered to Lucie Dreyfus."

"What does that mean?"

"She's going to ask me to write about the…"

Interrupting, and alarmed, I said, "You can't be serious. Would you even consider it? You can't take this on."

"If not me, then who?"

"Then you're going to do it?" I nervously tapped my spoon against the cup.

"I haven't decided that yet. But I'm upset about the court-martial."

Confused, as I hadn't yet heard of the Esterhazy trial, I cocked my head and asked, "What are you referring to?"

He jolted up straight in the chair. "You haven't heard that Esterhazy asked for a court-martial? It must have lasted all of three minutes." Throwing his arms up in the air, "Now that's real justice for you!"

Concluding the decision was bad news, I said, "You saw the court record?"

"Heavens no! It will be locked up in perpetuity. What I know is that he asked for a court-martial to clear his name. Smart move for an imbecile, and one with no conscience. It's doubtful if he has any redeeming qualities."

"Zola," it was how I referred to him when I was in my fatherly mien, "you can't take this on. It will ruin you."

"Charles, I told you I don't know what I plan to do. She," referring to Lucie Dreyfus, "hasn't approached me yet. It might not even happen."

Zola kept me abreast of his involvement with Dreyfus's wife. Alas, my hope that he would...or could...stay silent on the matter was dashed in short order. The next day Lucie Dreyfus made contact with Zola (through a mutual friend) that she wanted to meet with him. He set up an appointment to see her the following day. That night he slept fitfully, swirling in indecision as sweat poured from his nightshirt. Knowing he would be called upon to help, he contemplated the best way to make known the facts surrounding the Dreyfus injustice. His thoughts went to communications he had had with the president of France, Felix Faure. President Faure was reputed to be a reasonable and fair man, and a person of high esteem with whom Zola had good rapport.

Zola told me he knew what he had to do and with whom he wanted to consult—his friend Georges Clemenceau—before attempting anything with Faure or meeting with Lucie Dreyfus. Clemenceau had served in politics, having been elected five times to the National Assembly. When not involved in public service, Clemenceau did journalistic work. He was a stellar, fearless advocate for truth and justice, as was Zola.

It was fortuitous for Zola that Clemenceau had been defeated for his chamber seat in the 1893 election and had restricted his political activities to return to journalism. By the end of 1897, he was owner and editor of the Paris daily newspaper *L'Aurore*, and had immense respect for Zola's writing. Their friendship and journalistic work was a collectively powerful voice for fact and sound reason. If Zola was determined to make a public statement about this Dreyfus injustice, at least he had a well-respected colleague beside him and a reputable newspaper to publish his work. But would either be enough to protect him?

The truth is on the march and nothing will stop it.

Émile Zola

Chapter Ten

Before his meeting with Lucie Dreyfus, Zola consulted with Clemenceau. Zola had an idea for how to approach exposing the mountain of information. I remember him telling me that was when the word "libel" came up. Interestingly it had the opposite effect of discouraging him; it motivated him. I recall the conversation he had with Clemenceau very well.

"You risk libel."

"Yes, and so do you, my friend," said Zola.

"It is our fallback position." They both understood that if Zola wrote the article and Clemenceau published it in his newspaper, nothing might come of it. If one or both were sued for libel, however, then the contents of the article would be admissible in the trial, opening the door for the court to request the full record of Esterhazy's court-martial. To expose Esterhazy's misdeeds would exonerate Dreyfus.

"Are you willing to risk that the burden will most likely fall on you?" Clemenceau asked.

"It is the cost of freedom of the press. It is the cost for maintaining my soul. In taking up this cause, as with all my writing, I pledge to tell the truth, in full—the truth about Dreyfus's trial, about the real traitor, and the evil cover-up. Vindictive hatred must be exposed!"

"Then write your article and let me see it."

"First I have an appointment with Lucie Dreyfus."

"Are you going to tell her about what you plan to write?"

"No. No one can know but us, and perhaps my confidant Charles, whom I trust like a father. To speak to anyone about this is to risk suppression, even imprisonment on some trumped-up charge."

"True."

That Zola entrusted this information to me heightened the bond between us, an honor to last for the rest of my days. The words "like a father" nourished me.

When we arrived at the quiet place in the French countryside not far from the city, Lucie Dreyfus and her brother-in-law Mathieu were already waiting at a table. Zola asked me to come along to listen to what he might miss and give my perspective.

When Mrs. Dreyfus's downcast eyes met Zola's, they lit up with hope. In her hand was a piece of paper with handwriting on it and I wondered if they were notes she had brought to discuss with Zola. Mathieu stood and extended his hand to us. When the introductions were finished I took a closer look at the paper and caught sight of a very personal, "When will I be able to kiss you?" My heart grew heavy as I realized she carried a love letter from her husband, like a good luck charm. She was calm when we began speaking. "Thank you for coming today, Mr. Zola." Taking in a deep breath, she appeared at a loss for where to begin.

Mathieu looked at Lucie's eyes welling with tears then to what she held in her hand. Visibly straining to stay composed he held his torso high and said, "I have come with my sister-in-law because of our great respect for you, Mr. Zola. You have shown honor and integrity in your writing."

Zola, in his wise and sensitive way, nodded and remained silent, inviting what they needed to communicate.

When Lucie finally spoke, my body lightened. In her voice was what I recognized as a great love that would sacrifice all. "Mr. Zola, the evidence has come to us that proves my husband's innocence." Tears running down her cheeks, she continued, "But the courts will do nothing about it."

When she reached for her handkerchief, Mathieu interjected, matter-of-factly, "The army." Clearly cautious of finding his footing with Zola and not to denigrate the military, he lowered his voice. "We are at a great disadvantage against its might."

For the first time in many minutes, Zola said impassively, "I understand."

I sat quietly observing the tension in Mathieu's face, his taut lips and pulled-tight forehead. They must have held back an ocean of anger and frustration.

Lucie's shoulders relaxed as Mathieu continued. She intently listened and when he was finished said she felt this was their last-ditch effort. "If not you, Mr. Zola, then who? Who would take up our cause?" she asked. They both felt there was no one else with the ethics and strength, the popularity of voice, as well as respect from people in political positions. "You are a man of honor, Mr. Zola, like my husband," she said, caressing the love letter.

"I will consider what you have told me today and your request." Zola patted Mathieu's arm, saying, "I will get back to you with my decision."

As we walked out of earshot, he asked, "What do you think, Charles?"

Holding back my hesitation, I said, "We both know what you are going to do."

That was the point at which I knew what Zola would do, not just for righting the injustice done to one Jewish military officer, but for the most fundamental utilitarian reasoning—one man's action impacts all of us. This is how Zola lived, and how his thinking worked. In spite of my own discomfort, I knew then that there was nothing I could do to dissuade him. Would I live to regret never trying?

.

Let us seek and we shall find.

Émile Zola

Chapter Eleven

A stash of crinkled papers on my floor, a frustrated moan from Zola, and I knew we were in for a long night. To be safe, with peace and quiet, he asked to draft his article at my home. "Of course." I was happy to accommodate him and be current on the unfolding scene.

"How does this sound?" he asked, and without waiting for my answer began reading. "And it is to you, Mr. President, that I shall proclaim this truth."

To hear "Mr. President" out loud was sobering. It distressed me to contemplate what President Felix Faure's response would be. I nervously tapped my hand to my thigh as he continued to tell me what he wrote.

"Knowing your integrity, I am convinced that you do not know the truth," he read. "But to whom if not to you, the first magistrate of the country, shall I reveal the vile baseness of those who truly are guilty?"

How could I be so close to this man and not know the depth of his rage about this matter? Only when I heard the lack of euphemism and harsh words pour from him did I understand the degree of the impact this perversion of justice had had on Zola. Admiration for him mixed with my own cowardice. I had never thought of myself as spineless until he shared this with me and I knew I'd not have had the nerve to speak so honestly, with so much passion, or to make such a convincing case as he was doing. My face flushed red with heat. I excused myself to get something to drink. I couldn't help fearing for him.

When his voice started cracking and his throat went dry from reading aloud and he needed to rest, he handed me pages to read to myself. I sweat as I read, "At the root of it all is one evil man, Lt. Colonel du Paty de Clam, who was at the time a mere major. He is the entire Dreyfus case, and it can only be understood through an honest and thorough examination that reveals his actions and responsibilities. He appears to be the shadiest and most complex of creatures, spinning outlandish intrigues and stooping to the deceits of cheap novels. It was he who came up with the scheme of dictating the text of the bordereau to Dreyfus. He was the one who had had the idea of observing him in a mirror-lined room. And he was the one that Major Forzinetti caught carrying a shuttered lantern that he planned to throw open on the accused man while he slept, hoping that, jolted awake by the sudden flash of light, Dreyfus would blurt out his guilt. I need say no more. Let us seek and we shall find. I am stating simply that Major du Paty de Clam, as the officer of justice charged with the preliminary investigation of the Dreyfus case, is the first and most grievous offender in the ghastly miscarriage of justice that has been committed."

My hand cramped and I had to stop to shake it. Zola was outside getting fresh air. I knew I had to finish and tell him what I thought before he came back. The text continued with castigation. Accusations came forth of how Dreyfus was set up. No name was left out. No one went unscathed from the initial rush to accuse Dreyfus through to his court-martial. By the time I came to the part involving Lucie Dreyfus, I was on the edge of my chair.

I couldn't be prouder of what I read next, nor could I have imagined Zola including it in his indictment. I held the poor woman's image and that love letter in my mind as I read, "Ah, that first trial! What a nightmare it is for those who know its true details. Major du Paty de Clam had Dreyfus arrested and placed in solitary confinement. He terrorized Mrs. Dreyfus by telling her that if she talked, her husband would be ruined. Meanwhile, the unfortunate Dreyfus was tearing at his flesh and proclaiming his innocence."

Nothing was beyond mention as I ventured on, glued to the page. The words, the story that unfolded, were more compelling than Hugo's *Les Misérables* or Dickens' *A Tale of Two Cities.* I continued. "But now we see Dreyfus appearing before the court-martial. Behind closed doors, the utmost secrecy is demanded. Had a traitor opened the border to the enemy and driven the German Emperor straight to Notre Dame, the measures of secrecy and silence could not have been more stringent. The public was astounded; rumors flew of the most horrible acts, the most monstrous deceptions, lies that were an affront to our history. The public, naturally, was taken in. No punishment could be too harsh. The people clamored for the traitor to be publicly stripped of his rank and demanded to see him writhing with remorse. Could these things be true, these unspeakable acts, these deeds so dangerous that they must be carefully hidden to keep Europe from going up in flames? No! They were nothing but demented fabrications."

The facts were laid out: everything that had leaked, everything the Dreyfus family gave to Zola, and what had been learned from liberal political friends involved in secret conversations. All of it had to be presented because Zola knew that he was setting the stones for a court case, his own libel trial. In doing that, the facts that were needed to exonerate Dreyfus could be introduced.

Rapidly vacillating emotions moved through me as I focused on the facetious way Zola satirized Dreyfus's trumped-up crimes. A man languished on Devil's Island for knowing several languages, occasionally visiting his birthplace, working hard and striving to be well-informed—preposterous! Zola mocked the handwriting experts, who apparently could not agree. This further justified the pathetic ridiculousness of the case revolving around the bordereau, which lacked professional validation. I laughed at the brilliant innuendo but also knew it was going to anger the establishment.

I glanced down. "It is a lie, all the more odious and cynical in that its perpetrators are getting off free without even admitting it. They stirred up France, they hid behind the understandable commotion they had set off, and they sealed their lips while troubling our hearts and perverting our spirit. I know of no greater crime against the state." I'd read enough and needed a break. Zola was still outside.

Zola's pain pierced me and I couldn't help wondering what issues from his past had surfaced. My own wounds came forth, and I felt for what my friend must be experiencing. Feeling inadequate, I wondered if Zola's beloved father, François, was speaking from his grave to his son, to offer what I could not?

The thought is a deed. Of all deeds, she fertilizes the world most.

Émile Zola

Chapter Twelve

I found Zola sitting in my garden. Looking at the nearly full moon, I asked, "Do you need to return to your home for dinner?" The turmoil had suppressed my appetite but I knew I needed to eat. And so did he.

"I am not expected..." his head jerked in the direction of my fence. "What's that?" he stuttered.

"Relax." Referring to a scratching sound, "The neighbor's cat likes to sharpen his claws on the wood posts. How about that walk to the bistro down the road? We need to eat."

Omitting any mention of food, he nodded, "A walk sounds like a good idea." Rapidly stroking his beard, "How far did you get?" he asked, referring to his written indictment.

"I just started on the Esterhazy case," I laughed.

Quelling the edge in his tone, he made eye contact. "You find it humorous?"

"Tension. And look at you pulling at your beard. We could use a laugh."

"Yes, we could. That betraying pig of a man is something to scoff at."

"Do you plan to bring in Scheurer-Kestner?"

"Very gently. There is no need to chronicle the doubts and conclusions reached by him when I can take care of that myself."

"What about Piquart?"

"Most definitely. He is an integral part in the cover-up."

As we walked, Zola went on to detail what he had spared me from reading, starting with Mathieu Dreyfus denouncing Esterhazy as the real author of the bordereau. When Scheurer-Kestner handed over a request for the revision of the Dreyfus court-martial to the Minister of Justice, Esterhazy had panicked. The rest of that debacle was sealed information but one had to wonder who Esterhazy's protectors were.

"And you're going to name names?"

"Yes. Nothing will be left out." He went on to say, "Right down to the handpicked judges, the Minister of War, the War Office, and the Chief of Staff." What he told me he also intended to include buckled my knees. "And what a nest of vile intrigues, gossip, and destruction that sacred sanctuary that decides the nation's fate has become! We are horrified by the terrible light the Dreyfus affair has cast upon it all, this human sacrifice of an unfortunate man, a 'dirty Jew.' Ah, what a cesspool of folly and foolishness, what preposterous fantasies, what corrupt police tactics, what inquisitorial, tyrannical practices! What petty whims of a few higher-ups trampling the nation under their boots, ramming back down their throats the people's cries for truth and justice, with the travesty of state security as a pretext."

"You're not going to tone down any of that?"

"No," he adamantly responded.

Offering him support, I put an arm on his back and we continued in silence until the restaurant was before us. Thankfully, the walk gave us both some mental distance from the disquiet, and an appetite.

That night, while Paris slept, Zola paced and wrote. He stayed the night at my home too exhausted to overcome the inertia that afforded just enough energy to complete his thoughts and put them to paper. My sleep was fitful as I heard him shuffling about. I couldn't stop thinking of how his article would conclude and the impact it would have on Clemenceau. Would he read the harsh accusatory words and back down? I dared to follow the train of thought that ended in failure, with Dreyfus rotting on Devil's Island and Zola ruined professionally and personally.

The morning came and Zola appeared refreshed with a second wind. He was just concluding the final editing touches on his missive. Glancing up at my approach, he waved a stack of papers. "Will this be the watershed event we had hoped for?" He handed them to me. "Have a review of this."

I read by the sun coming through a crack in the curtained window. There was mention of Lt. Colonel Picquart being shipped off to Tunisia to an area where there was a great likelihood of him being massacred. I squirmed when I read, "It is a crime to poison the minds of the meek and the humble, to stoke the passions of reactionism and intolerance, by appealing to that odious anti-Semitism that, unchecked, will destroy freedom-loving France of the rights of man. It is a crime to exploit patriotism in the service of hatred, and it is, finally, a crime to ensconce the sword as the modern god, whereas all science is toiling to achieve the coming era of truth and justice."

I wanted to stand and cheer but the gravity of the situation held me back. Ambivalence over the mastery of Zola's writing and my devout respect for him as a man intermingled with fear—for him, for Dreyfus, for France. Again my heart sank when I read his direct address to the president. "It will leave an indelible stain on your presidency. I realize that you have no power over this case, that you are limited by the constitution and your entourage. You have, nonetheless, your duty as a man, which you will recognize and fulfill. As for myself, I have not despaired in the least of the triumph of right."

Zola concluded with the named accusations for those involved: Lt. Col. du Paty de Clam for "being the diabolical creator of this miscarriage of justice," several generals for their complicity (all specifically named), the handwriting experts (again, all named), the War Office for using the press to mislead the public in the cover-up of its wrongdoing, the first court-martial for violating the law by trying the accused with evidence kept secret from him, and the second court-marital for acquitting a guilty man with full knowledge of his guilt.

Bile rose in my throat when I read, "In making these accusations I am aware that I am making myself liable to articles 30 and 31 of the July 29 1881 law on the press making libel a punishable offense. I expose myself to that risk voluntarily." What he wanted, he said, was to "hasten the explosion of truth and justice." When Zola went on to espouse no ill will or hatred for those accused, that, in fact, he had never met them, I wanted to cry that it had all come to this.

If you shut up truth and bury it under the ground, it
will but grow, and gather to itself such explosive
power that the day it bursts through it will blow up
everything in its way.

Émile Zola

Chapter Thirteen

Clemenceau was at his desk when we arrived. The room remained quiet until he completed reading the lengthy article. When he was finished he looked at Zola with sad eyes. "You know what it means that you addressed the libel articles." He leaned back in his chair. "Are you sure you want to go ahead with this?"

Zola nodded affirmation.

"It will be the front page of tomorrow's edition of *L'Aurore.*"

Zola soberly replied, "There is no other way for the poor man."

"Then," Clemenceau replied, "it is on our shoulders," referring to himself as owner and Perrenx, the manager of the paper, and Zola. "If I am not named, and Perrenx is, I will ask my savvy attorney brother to join me in defending him on behalf of the paper."

§ § § §

On January 13, 1898, Émile Zola's communication to the President of France, entitled *J'Accuse...! LETTRE AU PRESIDENT DE LA REPUBLIQUE Par ÉMILE ZOLA,* appeared on the front page of the widely read international newspaper.

The letter caused quite a stir in France and abroad. The 4,000-word diatribe by the most popular writer in France, and my close friend, electrified Paris and rippled far and wide for days. Leading artists, writers, academics, and the intellectual class supported Zola's argument by making public statements such as, "The stakes are those of democracy and justice—due process, individual rights, and justice under the law." Those opposed to Dreyfus, the reactionary army and the Catholic Church, spewed hateful statements like, "Jews are faithless degenerates! They will destroy social stability and tradition."

Included among the voices were those of the Dreyfus family. "God bless you, Mr. Zola," Lucie wrote in a tear-stained thank you note to him.

The implication by Émile Zola of a conspiracy to frame Alfred Dreyfus infuriated General Jean-Baptiste Billot, the minister of war. A proud man, who had achieved a brilliant military career and received the Grand-Cross of the Légion d'Honneur, he would have none of it. We had heard secondhand that he puffed his chest and exclaimed, "How dare he accuse me! The military! The disrespectful, unlimited gall of that Jew-loving journalist! He will not get away with this!"

Days passed and Zola's head pounded as he waited for the axe to fall. Yelling, rock throwing, and disgruntled crowds confronted him in the street. Windows were broken in his carriage and his home with Alexandrine, necessitating police to come out in force to protect a journalist. He was guarded twenty-four hours a day. He tried to occupy himself with writing to no avail. He ended up filling his days with visitors bringing news. The word about town was that General Billot had ordered a libel suit brought against Zola and Perrenx. It was hard for me to ignore the dark cloud hanging over him as he tried to maintain his civility. "At least Clemenceau will be protected," he said to me.

Life was not normal and there was no use pretending that it was. The storm on the horizon loomed as we took to drink to divert our attention from the noisy, dangerous distractions outside Zola's home. Impatiently, we awaited the expected knock on the door. Several weeks later it came from a panting messenger, short of breath from running to deliver the message. Zola had been served. The court date was set for February 7, 1898. The clouds had been summoned, and that day they gushed a downpour.

§ § § §

The trial was held in the Court of Assizes of the Seine, the principal criminal court in France. Zola and Perrenx appeared in somber dress and mood. I found a seat in the back of the crowded room. The place went silent as Judge Delegorgue entered and sat. He looked towards Zola's attorney, Fernand Labori, and Perrenx's attorneys, Albert and Georges Clemenceau, then out at the crowd and said, "I notify the public that we shall not begin until all are seated. I likewise warn the public that every sort of manifestation, whether for or against the accused, is formally forbidden, and that at the first sign of disorder I shall order the courtroom cleared. Please consider this said once and for all, for I shall not repeat it."

The other members of the court were attorneys Lault and Bousquet. The Attorney General, Van Cassel, appeared for the prosecution.

The usual dialogue ensued between the judge and Zola.

"Your name?"

"Émile Zola."

"Your profession?"

"Man of letters."

"Your age?"

"Fifty-eight years."

"Your residence?"

"21 bis, Rue de Bruxelles."

The drawing of the jury then proceeded, which included merchants, a roof builder, clerks, a proprietor, a seedsman, a leather dresser, a linen maker, and a butcher. I looked at them, all men, seemingly ordinary citizens, and couldn't help wondering what their political and religious affiliations were. How would they feel about a prestigious writer coming to the aid of a Jewish officer? Feeling ill at ease, I shifted my attention away from the group of men who held my friend's fate in their hands.

Next began the reading of the documents in the case by the clerk, the one of interest being the complaint of General Billot, referring to Zola's letter, upon which the suit was brought. When he was done, Attorney General Van Cassel took the floor to make his statement of the case. He summarized the accusation against the Minister of War, and smugly asked the jury, "Did the first Council of War act in obedience to orders in acquitting Major Esterhazy?"

I cringed in my seat when I saw one of the jurors gently nod his head in agreement with Van Cassel. "I ask, then, that the accused may not be authorized to attempt proof thereof, either by documents or by testimony." There it was, the request to suppress the documents that Zola desperately wanted entered into the record on behalf of Dreyfus. I sat up straighter, waiting.

Zola's attorney addressed the court with, "I am not much astonished, gentlemen, at the difficulties that Mr. Zola meets in this affair, and I expect that this incident, which is the first, will not be the last. We expected that the opposition would offer to you and impose upon us a restricted discussion. Such was the desire of the Minister of War, and it was his right. It will be ours, at a certain moment, to ask what could have been the underlying reasons for the exercise of this right under the circumstances in which the Minister of War has made use of it." Labori relaxed his manner, and so did I when he continued to read Zola's accusations concerning the Minister of War, among others, and that evidence would be presented as proof. "Therefore," he said, "Mr. Attorney General, let us say no more of exceptions." He then submitted a formal motion that the court authorize the introduction of evidence on all matters referred to in Zola's public letter.

The judge rendered an adverse decision on the motion, claiming it was not directly connected with the matter of the trial. Another blow was that the judge had a letter from the Keeper of Seals, saying that the Minister of War, General Billot, had not been authorized to respond to his summons. Several other key witnesses had similar letters or medical excuses.

My pulse sped up as the proceedings continued in the competent hands of Labori, where most of the defense attention went. When it became known that du Paty de Clam wouldn't be appearing, Labori proclaimed, "This is the first time that I have known witnesses to be judged according to the utility of their evidence. Mr. du Paty de Clam is not sick, nor is he detained, so far as I know, by the duties of his military office. He does not know upon what points he is to be examined, or what we shall ask him. It is his duty to appear in this case. We have to question him as well on matters of fact as on matters of morals pertaining exclusively to the Esterhazy case, and not at all to the Dreyfus case. Under these circumstances it is indispensable that he appear at this bar." He further mentioned that if he needed to take shelter behind professional secrecy, then he could do that but, "Even then it is our right to make a motion before the court, challenging the law upon which no answer is acceptable by law. If it be the case and closed doors are necessary, then we shall have them."

The rest of the day proceeded in a similar manner, with the defense calling witnesses and the judge proclaiming that, for each witness, he had a letter providing an "acceptable excuse" not to appear. Labori asked that everything be clearly stated in the record (evidence, whether the witnesses were ordered not to appear or if they simply chose to be excused), so that when his motions were decided on the next day, he might ask for a postponement of the trial. The message was clear: play games with him, he'd play right back. But the game he was playing involved my dear friend's life.

I have but one passion: to enlighten those who have been kept in the dark, in the name of humanity, which has suffered so much and is entitled to happiness.

Émile Zola

Chapter Fourteen

The second day of the trial began with a letter from Esterhazy stating that because of the acquittal rendered in his favor, he did not feel justified in responding to Mr. Zola's summons. To this Albert Clemenceau stood and demanded he appear to be questioned on behalf of the newspaper *L'Aurore*.

Frustrated and tired of the nonsense, Labori made his move and called Mrs. Dreyfus to the stand. Wearing black from neck to feet and appearing pale, Lucie rose and slowly walked to the front of the courtroom. As she was being sworn in, a man next to me whispered, "Dirty Jew." My gut knotted.

She sat in the witness chair and waited while the judge and Labori argued back and forth about the relevancy of the first question to her concerning what she thought of Zola's good faith. "What has that to do with this case?" the judge demanded to know. It was clear he was about to refuse to let her answer it.

Labori argued that it spoke to Zola's good faith in coming forth. Zola then interjected, "I ask to be allowed here the liberty that is accorded thieves and murderers. They can defend themselves, summon witnesses and ask them questions, but every day I am insulted in the street. They break my carriage windows, they roll me in the mud, and an unclean press treats me as a bandit. I have the right to prove my good faith, my probity, my honor."

The judge glared at Zola who was sitting at the defendant's table. Turning to Labori, he responded, "I remind you of the terms of the decree rendered yesterday by the court, the provisions of Article 11 of the law of 1881, and the terms of your summon. Let us not depart therefrom. Any question outside of these limits will not be put by me. Let that be well understood. It is useless to recur to the matter."

The Press Law of 1881, referenced by the judge, had a limitation in Article 11, which imposes legal obligations on publishers and criminalizes certain specific behaviors, particularly concerning defamation. By citing this law, the judge had stated the legal ground for narrowing the boundaries of what he would allow into the record.

Not to be deterred, Zola repeated, "I ask to be treated here as well as thieves and murderers. All accused persons are entitled to prove their probity, their good faith, and their honor."

His attorney followed promptly with, "Will you permit me to point out the bearing of my questions? Mr. Zola has made two assertions. He has asserted that the Council of War of 1894 convicted, in the person of ex-Captain Dreyfus, an innocent man by illegal methods. And that the second council acquitted a guilty man."

Lucie Dreyfus, on the verge of tears, sat quietly, waiting to see if she would be allowed to answer questions. One fortuitous mention of Alfred Dreyfus and the door would be open. As the tension rose, the judge continued to shut down motions for questions to Mrs. Dreyfus.

He finally put his foot down when asked if he would accept any questions involving good faith, to which he said, "Anything concerning the Dreyfus case, no." Stunning me, this non sequitur highlighted the bias of the judge that had set the mood in the court. Snickers and jeers came from those in favor of the judge's prejudice while the few liberals shook their heads in disgust.

Lucie Dreyfus gasped. A pound of the gavel to quiet the commotion sounded a shock wave through the poor woman, and she appeared to struggle to regain her composure. Labori glanced over to her as he asked the judge, "Will you permit me, in our common interest, to ask you, then, what practical means you see by which we may ascertain the truth?"

With pursed lips, his response came back, "That does not concern me."

Unbelievable! I dug my foot in the floor to subdue my frustration that this trial was getting nowhere. There seemed no hope for justice in France for Dreyfus, for Zola, or any unfairly treated person. I worried how Zola was holding up under this charade of judiciary integrity.

Labori, containing his furious reaction, asked the court's permission to put questions before Mrs. Dreyfus. "I would like to ask her," he said, "to describe Major du Paty de Clam's visit to her house. Did he utter the grossest insults against her husband? Did he forbid her to speak of the arrest of her husband to anyone, including family? What does she think of Mr. Zola's good faith? Does she consider the measure taken against her husband to be illegal?" There were more, but when those in the courtroom responded to the reading of these questions with hostility, Labori shouted, "If you think you can prevent me from doing my duty, you are mistaken. I am embarrassed only when I am applauded. Let them howl! It is all one to me."

"Silence!" said the judge with another pound of the gavel. "Denied."

Mrs. Dreyfus did not speak before Zola was called forth to be questioned. Crestfallen, yet holding her head high, she walked back to her seat in the audience. I wanted to weep for her.

Zola walked past the two court judges sitting before Judge Delegorgue, his attention towards the jury. Movement in chairs, coughs, and shuffling papers stilled as he stepped into the witness box. Continuing to look at the jurors, he said, "Gentlemen of the jury, to you will I address myself. I am not an orator, I am a writer, but unfortunately…"

Impatiently Delegorgue interrupted him with, "You should address the court!"

Zola gripped his hands together to stop their shaking, and slowed his response as he turned to the judge and apologized. He went on to say he was not accustomed to public speaking, and was likely to use words without a clear legal meaning that caused his being misunderstood. He expressed his hope that a sentence or two would not be taken out of context of all he said, referring to the accusations in *J'Accuse*.

Smiling, I thought to myself that Zola's humility to quell the judge's anger was a smart move on his part. It worked mildly as the judge's tone softened, but Zola was not allowed to answer questions posed to him from any of the defense attorneys. When he left the stand I looked at the ceiling and prayed that the heavens beyond would open and cast a better light on the situation. When Scheurer-Kestner took the stand and was asked about Esterhazy being the guilty culprit, my emotions once again lifted, until the judge proclaimed, "Mr. Scheurer-Kestner, you are to tell us of Major Esterhazy, but I beg you not to say anything of the Dreyfus case, concerning which we will not hear a word."

The political jockeying and maneuvering continued with the defense attorneys doing their best; however, their efforts were in vain as the judge continued to reject their motions and questions. That is how the rest of the day went, leaving those of us on Dreyfus's side feeling deflated and hopeless. Meeting later with Zola, Labori told him not to worry about what seemed like a closed door.

"You see a way to open it?"

"Yes," he smiled.

Straight-faced, Zola queried, "Dare I ask?"

"Émile, more of the same. Sooner or later, hopefully sooner, legal shades of grey will favor us. And Dreyfus."

"Yes, Dreyfus. That's the whole point," Zola said, patting Labori on the back.

As we walked away from the courthouse surrounded by guards, I asked Zola, "Do you regret any of this?"

"Yes and no," he answered. "I won't lie about my nervous ambivalence, but I will never regret doing right by another human being."

I shuddered to think that Zola's noble efforts might not be worth the eventual price he will have to pay in the end. A price we may all incur for having assisted him to defend a traitor. If the facts are never brought to light about Alfred Dreyfus's injustice will we all look like guilty accomplices? If so then what?

Dwell on this, because this is the germ of it all, whence the true crime would emerge, that horrifying miscarriage of justice that has blighted France

Émile Zola

Chapter Fifteen

When the trial resumed the next day, Scheurer-Kestner took the stand again and the proceedings started with a ray of hope. Tired from a fitful night's sleep, an overly active mind, and too much imbibing, it was hard for me to focus, but I snapped to attention when I heard mention of letters. They included information that Scheurer-Kestner had from Lt. Colonel Picquart that stated the authorship of the bordereau had been mistakenly attributed to Alfred Dreyfus.

I bit my lower lip and prayed.

Scheurer-Kestner went on to say that Picquart made haste to inform his seniors, including General Gonse, showing them the bordereau and Major Esterhazy's handwriting. My headache lifted when he said, "I was convinced by reading the data that Piquart was correctly paving the way for a revision of the Dreyfus trial."

The muffled din in the courtroom grew louder, and the judge pounded the gavel. "Quiet in the courtroom! Another outburst and I will have it cleared." Turning back to the witness seat, he told Scheurer-Kestner to continue.

"It seems to me indispensable, in order to enlighten the jurors, that I should read this correspondence to them."

"No, that is not possible," said the judge.

The Attorney General jumped on the judge's comment with a loud, "General Gonse and Lieutenant-Colonel Picquart have been summoned. They will testify concerning the letters, if they see fit."

Everyone with any intelligence who'd been following the trial knew this was a delaying tactic, and that if and when they did make it to the witness stand, nothing concerning Dreyfus's innocence would be introduced. *Damnation!*

Labori countered with a plea that Scheurer-Kestner be allowed to read the letters. The shut door creaked open, millimeter by millimeter, with articles of the law cited by the defense attorneys to introduce them. The judge countered every plea, until finally a spark ignited and out came, "Offer your motion. But after all, if Scheurer-Kestner, instead of reading them, wishes to say what they contain, he may do so."

Scheurer-Kestner then repeated the substance of the letters.

My lungs cleared and I tried to keep the smile from my face. I wanted to stand and scream, *finally!* More back and forth continued and I could feel Zola's relief when Scheurer-Kestner said that he was an old friend of General Billot, the Minister of War. Filled with emotion, Scheurer-Kestner went on to say, "I addressed General Billot with the utmost familiarity, and almost wept in his arms as I begged him, in the name of France, to take the matter up, concerning the false claims against Dreyfus."

I caught sight of Mathieu Dreyfus sitting alone, and wondered where Lucie Dreyfus was. We listened to Scheurer-Kestner. "The conversation that I had with General Billot was a long one. Yes, I pleaded with him to give his best attention to this matter, which otherwise was likely to become extremely serious. 'It is incumbent upon you,' I said to him, 'to take the first steps, make a personal investigation; do not trust the matter to anyone. There are bundles of documents in certain offices. Send for them. Use no intermediary. If you will promise to do this, I pledge myself to maintain silence until I know the result.' As I left, General Billot asked me to say nothing to anyone."

The jurors paid close attention to Scheurer-Kestner's testimony and I think I noticed one smack his lips in dislike when he heard him say, "I agreed, but on one condition: two hours, I said, are all that is necessary for this investigation. I give you a fortnight, and during that fortnight I will not take a step." Scheurer-Kestner looked distraught as he continued. "Now, during that fortnight I was dragged in the mud, pronounced a dishonest man, treated as a wretch, covered with insults, and called a German and a Prussian."

Although no definitive data was submitted as to the bundles of letters that Scheurer-Kestner had asked General Billot to investigate, the crack in the door had widened, and I slept better that night.

§ § § §

The fourth day of the trial started out with a surprise. The judge stated that in refusing to hear Mrs. Dreyfus concerning Mr. Zola's good faith, he assumed questions would be directed to the Dreyfus case. Therefore, he said, "The court desires the defense to specify whether the questions will be put in regard to the Dreyfus case or the Esterhazy case."

Labori gave Zola a look and from behind the table I could see him give Zola a gentle pat on the back, signifying this was good news. Labori responded, "I do not understand. Since Mr. Zola is accused of a crime, we seek to show that his action was done in good faith and not out of criminal intent." He continued to address the judge. "We maintain that Zola's actions were bona fide, and in asking the witness what she thinks, we cannot separate the interconnection between the Dreyfus case and the Esterhazy case."

The judge went on to say that he would question Mrs. Dreyfus on the matter of the Esterhazy case. Since she was not present in the court that day, the proceedings continued with the calling of other witnesses. The first witness the next day was supposed to be Mrs. Dreyfus. But once again, Mathieu was alone.

Labori stood, looked around the room, and waited for the whispering to stop before he told the judge, "Mrs. Dreyfus will not be attending. I excused her in view of a letter that I will read." Without pause, Lucie Dreyfus spoke that day through Labori's impassioned voice:

"Dear Master: I answered to the call of my name at Tuesday's hearing, in spite of my great agitation. I made the effort because I hoped to express to the court and the jury my deep gratitude to, and my admiration for, Mr. Zola, who, obeying the voice of his conscience, has sacrificed himself for justice and truth with a sublime disdain of the insults and threats, which he has drawn upon himself. I hoped also to declare my absolute faith in my husband's innocence—an innocence which, I am convinced, will be established before long—and also my sincere gratitude to you, dear master, who display so much courage and talent to secure the triumph of the truth. The anguish of these current proceedings, added to all that I have suffered for three years, has put me in a condition in which I could not continue to endure. Permit me, then, to absent myself from the court and accept, I beg of you, the expression of my most distinguished sentiments. L. Dreyfus. February 10, 1898."

A man sitting two seats over from me smirked and under his breath declared, "Of course she wouldn't come to defend her Jew-traitor husband." I wanted to hit him.

The winds were shifting. I could feel it despite the acrimony of many people present. Still, I couldn't help but worry. Would this change in the air be enough to save my friend, and more importantly, his faith in all that is good in this life?

Ah, that first trial! What a nightmare it is for all who know it in its true details.

Émile Zola

Chapter Sixteen

Miserably cold and stormy weather prevailed on the sixth day of the trial. Zola moved on ahead to talk with Labori as I lingered in the hallway, trying to dry off before going in and taking a seat. Toned-down courtroom whispers were audible from two feet away. "That miserable man deserves what he got," someone said, referring to an earlier mention of Dreyfus. "Bringing the whole country to a standstill, Zola has a lot of nerve. And to throw away his reputation and acclaim to defend a traitor, he deserves to join him."

It was all I could do to contain my temper from speaking out or taking an action. I wanted to yell from the top of my lungs that this was a hall of justice where facts should be heard and citizens be judged on the truth, not on gossip. I couldn't help thinking that the two trials of the century, dividing France, were nothing more than rumormongers' sensational cover-ups. They were vulgar displays of the hatred that lived in their anti-

Semitic hearts. That kind of hatred is the vilest, for it is not content with mere gossip between the simpleminded, but spreads like infection unable to be contained, sullying what it comes in contact with. Yes, I wanted to scream *SHUT UP!* but I knew I would continue to keep my moral outrage to myself. My reticent nature causes me shame in comparison to Zola. I hide in his shadow, hold my tongue, and dare to do no more than offer him support. He tells me that I am courageous to stand by him. Zola sees altruism in me that I do not see in myself. When I look at men like him—true heroes who act magnanimously—I see that am in need of valor.

Feeling nauseated and intolerant of the pettiness, I went inside. Unrest filled the room as we waited for the judge to appear. Once he was at the bench, a hush came over the attendees. The silence was a welcome change from the earlier repugnant chatter.

The questions presented to the first witness, a military officer, were concerning the transfer of Lt. Colonel Piquart away from Paris. Whatever the trumped-up reason, the truth was that Piquart, a man of great integrity was exiled because he wanted to exonerate Captain Alfred Dreyfus. Nothing of significance surfaced for the record; stories and lies were all that came forth.

Volleying between the attorneys and judge continued. When Du Paty de Clam took the stand, he instantly defended himself as a man of honor who was dragged through the mud with false claims against him for his part in the cover-up. I thought it a sure sign of guilt that he should defend his innocence when nothing was even asked of him. His use of the words "French honor" made me sick.

When the judge responded with, "But there have been no questions," I wanted to laugh. Du Paty de Clam was a clown act.

More of the same nonsense continued. Witness after witness had nothing Labori deemed important to be admitted into the record. Zola's lawyer stated each time a useless witness wasted the court's time, for official documentation, "I never before saw an assize court like this. All means are sought here to prevent the light from being thrown on any important point of questioning. Therefore, answers are not forthcoming!"

Toward midafternoon, testimony came up about how Mathieu Dreyfus had lodged a formal complaint with the Minister of War accusing Esterhazy of being the author of the bordereau. The witness was given a complete file with documented handwriting samples, among other accusatory information. Finally, the bundle of documents that Scheurer-Kestner brought up could be introduced.

The Attorney General objected.

I learned forward in anticipation for the judge's decision.

Again this was not entered into the official record. To my deepest respect and amazement, unscathed Labori, in a calm, intelligent, determined manner, continued hammering questions at witnesses. Despite his brilliant attempts, the judge countered with, "Say nothing of Dreyfus" to one witness after another for twelve days, and didn't stop until the testimonies ended and summations began. The documents introduced by Scheurer-Kestner never made it into the final transcript.

On day thirteen, February 21, 1898, Attorney General Van Cassel started with, "Gentlemen of the jury, a man well-known in letters goes in search of a militant newspaper, comes to an understanding with it, and publishes an article which shows either irresponsibility or shamelessness. He declares that a Council of War has rendered a verdict in obedience to orders. 'Let them prosecute me in the assize court, if they dare,' Zola writes. Well, here we are," he pointed a finger at Zola. "But where are your proofs, those precise and irrefutable proofs that the Council of War has rendered a verdict in obedience to orders? During the twelve sessions that you have just passed through not once has this question, the only one before us, been posited. You have attempted no proof."

What the blazes is he talking about? My mind was a blank with the illogic of his argument. But then, with the pertinent evidence of collusion withheld, I knew he didn't need to say much to make his point and win over the jury. Zola's head followed Van Cassel's movement as he continued with, "The experts in the Esterhazy case worked separately, and arrived by different methods at identical conclusions."

It was all I could do to stay in my seat listening to this maddening diatribe of drivel. I wanted to pull at my graying hair and protest to the gentlemen of the jury, *What about honest facts and justice? You all heard that everything was thrown out!* I knew that although their ears took in the inadmissible truth, there sat before us twelve men, with puffed out, proud French chests ready to defend the good of the country—the military. Who was Zola to them? Surely not a symbol of what was right and decent, the best of the human condition. I just prayed that the truth would win out in the end, whenever that might be. It certainly didn't seem to be heading in that direction.

Just when it appeared the bottom had been reached, stealing any thread of hope, hell opened up, and from Van Cassel out came, "Alfred Dreyfus alone was in a position to procure the documents concerning the national defense that are enumerated in the bordereau. General de Pellieux and General Gonse are in a position to know more about that than anybody else. After what they have told you, it is impossible to doubt. But I shall say no more about the Dreyfus case. It would be a violation of the authority of the subject being judged."

What the defense attorneys had been attempting for days on end, to enter Dreyfus's case into the record, was alluded to, naked and bare of any facts. And if that wasn't enough, Van Cassel threw in, "Dreyfus belongs to a rich and powerful family, which continues to keenly feel the deep sorrow of having seen one of its members convicted of high treason. Their campaign has been carefully prepared. It began in the press before ending in parliamentary incidents and judicial proceedings." Van Cassel's calculating tonal indictment of the Dreyfus family as manipulative was a ploy to make Zola look like their puppet, further discrediting him.

The coffin was nailed shut and it didn't matter what Labori or the Clemenceau brothers brought before the jurors, for in their summations they were not allowed to include the Dreyfus case. The twelve men walked to the room of decision and returned to the court in thirty-five minutes, wearing expressions of pride and dignity. Deluded beliefs filled their empty heads, as the foreman rose and said, "On my honor and my conscience, the declaration of the jury is: As concerns Perrenx, yes, by a majority vote. As concerns Zola, yes, by a majority vote."

Cries of, "Long live the army, long live France, down with the insulters, to the door with Jews, and death to Zola!" broke out in the room.

Zola slumped in his chair and sadly lamented, "These people are cannibals."

The court then retired to deliberate upon the sentences. Returning a few minutes later, it condemned Mr. Perrenx, the gérant of *L'Aurore*, to an imprisonment of four months and the payment of a fine of three thousand francs. Upon Émile Zola it inflicted the maximum penalty of one year in prison and a fine of three thousand francs.

Zola took his sentencing quietly as a few supporters surrounded him. He was secretly removed from the court and taken to a friend's house, where he spent the night.

Alone with my thoughts, I pondered where we were when this debacle started. Back then I hadn't envisioned that "our" France would be so cold-hearted. What would it take for her to thaw?

Civilization will not attain its perfection until the last stone from the last church falls on the last priest.

Émile Zola

Chapter Seventeen

Disheartened, I walked with Labori away from the boisterous commotion coming from the courthouse. The symbol of justice for all had become a pathetic parody. Hatred lived in the fading voices we distanced ourselves from. The day was crisp and clear with an after-rain freshness lingering in the air. When the sun broke through the clouds, we didn't feel the usual invigoration from such a beautiful day. It was tainted by the ugliness of the words yet echoing in our minds—"Death to Zola!" and "Lock him away with the Jew traitor." If that wasn't bad enough, the vileness expanded in more than one person with, "Kill the Jews who are polluting our beloved France!"

The irony of hearing the word *beloved* in the same sentence with *kill the Jews* made my skin crawl. "Where does this hatred come from?" I asked Labori, not really expecting anything to be said in response to my rhetorical question.

Labori mumbled, "Clerical influence."

"Excuse me?" I questioned.

The shadow lines on his handsome face darkened. "The roars that started with the publication of *J'Accuse...*" he didn't finish the sentence.

Tilting my head, I squinted to avoid the direct sunlight and gave him a look. "I don't understand. What do you mean?"

Responding to my puzzlement, he said, "When over three-hundred-thousand copies of the paper went out that day, the uproar in the streets wasn't the only violent protestation. The few papers that reprinted the letter infuriated the bulk of the press who opposed Dreyfus. The men of the cloth threw off their disguises and had the papal nuncio's henchman call formally for the government in the Chamber of Deputies to put a stop to the attacks on the honor of the army. That is what prompted our friend's prosecution."

Sinking into myself, I looked at the ground as we continued to walk. Labori went on, "The blood of two men," referring to Zola and Dreyfus, "wasn't enough for them. The Archbishop of Paris suggested that all members of the Dreyfus family and Jewish leaders who were fueling the schism of France also be indicted."

"For which," I said, "Zola and Perrenx became the heads on a pike."

"Yes. The situation was inflamed by the riots in parts of France where priestly cause had strong influence: Lyons,

Marseilles, Notre Dame de la Garde, and especially Nantes, which had sent the anti-Semitic Pontbriand as a representative in parliament." His dry throat cracking, Labori continued to tell me that the extent of anti-Semitic hatred was seen in the violence in French Algeria where Jews were beaten, wounded, and killed. "Their houses and shops were ransacked and burnt."

My legs felt heavy and I slowed my motion. "I didn't know it was that bad."

Labori looked back to me and said, "That gives you an idea of the acrimony we are facing. Because many high-ranking in the army were called as witnesses, the bitterness intensified."

"Why?" I asked.

"Overwhelming portions of officers in the French army belong to devout Catholic families, often aristocratic and royalist with great influence. There was prejudice and sizeable resentment against Alfred Dreyfus from the beginning of his enrollment in the War College. But then the animosity was talked about behind closed doors."

I was still reeling from the shock of recent events surrounding the trial. What Labori had just said shook me to my core and I began to realize how dangerous this undertaking was. I felt embarrassed over my ignorance. How could I be deluded into believing any good could come from Zola writing his letter and going against the army? And the Catholic Church?

That day in the library several weeks back, when I tried to gain an understanding about the anti-Semitism in France, I thought I had grasped it. I couldn't have been further from comprehending what prejudice and persecution do to the hearts of men fighting for a cause that they fervently believe in. *Where was the love I had learned from the nuns? My heart tells me it is the love of God.*

I felt ill. The only mitigation to this horrible situation was Zola's friends who would protect him. One friend, Jacques, remained at Zola's side with a six-shooter in readiness should anyone try to harm him. Police were also on guard.

Undeterred, Labori filed for a review with the appeals court. The days leading up to his appearance were tense, and once again as the citizens of Paris slept, Zola paced. He relived the stressful events daily, endured more rock-throwing through the windows of his home, and welcomed the increased police protection. The painful irony was that Esterhazy walked the streets a free man, continuing his debauchery, and gambled away his available funds, all under the protection of military might.

I often wondered if the turmoil was worth it. Zola told me it was. Knowing now how this has progressed, I don't know that I would have advised him to enter into the peril in the first place. I doubt I'll ever stop wondering if the price Zola paid, and most likely will continue to pay, was worth defending an innocent man. Will my dear friend ever be able to walk with his head held high in this country for which he has given so much of himself? For a man who has clung to the ideal of justice so loyally, will she ever so cling to him? God help Zola. God help Dreyfus. God help France. God help us all.

If I cannot overwhelm with my quality, I will overwhelm with my quantity.

Émile Zola

Chapter Eighteen

Crowds continued to gather outside Zola's residence and I was happy to see that the police warded them off. Shouts of "Down with the Jews" came from demonstrators in front of liberal newspaper offices. I continued to be repulsed by the abundant hypocrisy and cowardice that existed in certain political and bourgeois circles. The exceptions were educated critical thinkers like Zola, who were disgusted with the Esterhazy court-martial. For the first time, members of the Institute of France, professors at the Paris faculty of medicine, provincial faculty members, and many other reputable scientists and literary men declared they were in favor of a revision of the Dreyfus case, adding to the already existing support. As the balance of power slowly shifted, Jew-haters, the army, and the clergy pursued means of suppressing anything to shine a light on the facts that could ultimately free Alfred Dreyfus.

It wasn't enough that the German Foreign Secretary declared that no relationship existed between Dreyfus and Germany (with similar declarations from the Italian and Austrian governments). Even diplomatic agents of France abroad shared that view, but nothing could check the absurdity of French chauvinism and stubborn government vanity. No matter how many times I heard the same arguments against our case, they still shocked me as insane and grossly unjust. It served Zola well that the courts and chancelleries of Europe knew of Esterhazy's guilt and that the foreign press shared that view. Compassion for Zola began to pour in from all over the world and he was grateful for the support. But it still felt like a slap in his patriotic face that he wasn't supported close to home, where doll figures of him hanging from a noose were burned in effigy and verbal manure was slung at him from every corner, including garnering him the label "the Italian." I wanted to take down those dolls and throw them in the garbage.

§ § § §

The documents from Zola's first trial were sent to the appeals court. They were slimmer than if more witnesses had come forth to testify. While we waited, Zola reminded me that nearly a hundred witnesses—ministers, officers, senators, diplomats, journalists, and handwriting experts—were summoned, with great and successful efforts to scare them off from attending. Their names were published in newspapers with threatening letters sent to them should they show up at the trial. For the ones that did appear—speculation included members of the jury—revenge would follow them were they to acquit "the Italian."

"What does that all mean with regards to the appeals court?" I asked Zola.

"Hopefully they will overturn Judge Delegorgue's decision. That's why Labori kept repeating for the record the excuses given by so many witnesses. His protestations of unfairness and the disallowing of entering things into the record have been documented. The transcript presented to the Court of Cassation should add up to an unfair trial."

"That would be a great relief," I replied. "If the court turns in your favor, let us hope that the noise outside your home here settles down."

"I can live with the noise if justice is served," said Zola.

As the case was moving up in the calendar of the Court of Cassation, nationalists and clerical leaders continued large-scale demonstrations to foil any of our attempts at justice for Dreyfus, Zola, or Jewish sympathizers. These anti-Semitic men congregated en masse around the court to protest, virtually unobstructed. Friends of Zola and Dreyfus volunteered to offer more protection. In addition to Jacques, others carried guns, putting the police on edge. I had my uncomfortable moments with Jacques and his compatriots carrying firearms. But for the most part I felt relieved that Zola was protected as these were tough times and the nationalists were surely armed.

The army hierarchy, clergy, and anti-Semites did not relent in their battle to reinforce their story, one the populace already believed: Dreyfus was guilty of treason. Anyone who begged to differ was faced with overwhelming contradicting voices. As the days grew closer to the date set for the appeals court to review the case, tensions continued to escalate. Zola was at his wits' end. It was not safe to be out in the streets, but he insisted he needed fresh air and a change of scenery. He went for a ride, accompanied by an armed entourage and me. He needed to get out of his carriage, and, as he told me, feel the earth beneath his feet. Courageous and defiant, it proved to be a foolish and near fatal move. Although surrounded by his friends, a group of men overtook him, lifted him to a parapet above the Seine, and were about to toss him in when we rescued him. After that, Labori insisted that Zola travel in a coach, accompanied by police on bicycles. Even then, he continued to be pursued by hostile mobs.

Zola's passion for truth and justice surmounted the opposition's aggressive attempts, and he swore to us that day by the Seine, "I will continue to write, to speak, to show up, in the name of what is right."

If only he knew the cost of his tenacity.

The fate of animals is of greater importance to me than the fear of appearing ridiculous; it is indissolubly connected with the fate of men.

Émile Zola

Chapter Nineteen

Located in the Palais de Justice building in Paris, the Court of Cessation is one of France's courts of last resort, having jurisdiction over review in determining miscarriages of justice. As the court of final appeal for civil and criminal cases, its main purpose is to evaluate the lower court rulings for legal or procedural errors. The appellant must obtain the court's permission before an appeal can be deliberated. It may support or set aside lower court rulings. New evidence to the case being submitted is not admissible. Published judgments are quite brief, including a statement of the case and a summary of the ruling. Labori explained all of this to Zola and me.

Filed by Labori, and Perrenx's attorneys, the appeal was accepted and put on the calendar for the Court of Cessation for April 2, 1898. That day dragged on as Zola tried to busy himself answering mail and tending to backlogged communications. A handful of friends, including myself, were at his side. Waiting for the panel of five judges to meet and render their decision was extremely trying on the nerves. A loud noise outside distracted us. Through the window I could see a police officer pounding his baton against the step's railing and, in an aggressive manner, telling a crowd forming to "Go home." When a young man, no older than in his early twenties, refused to obey and stepped toward him with a gun, the officer pounded it out of his hand with his stick.

The boy yelled, "Jew-lover deserves to rot in hell," as he rubbed his sore arm and left. When the officer reached for his gun, the rest of the crowd dispersed.

Acid rose to my throat when I heard a carriage approach the front of the house. Soon there was a knock on the door. Smiling, Labori entered waving a piece of paper, proclaiming, "Good news." He went to where Zola was standing, looked him square in the eyes, and told him, "They squashed the conviction."

"On what grounds?" asked Zola.

"The proceedings should have been initiated not by the Minister of War but by the court-martial that the libel was aimed at."

"Now what?" asked Zola.

"We wait to see if they will file another suit."

"And so the attrition continues." I regretted opening my mouth the minute I said it.

"Euphemistically speaking, yes," said Labori. "As long as it's conducted in court and we can fend off outside attackers and keep you safe," he said looking at Zola, "we can sustain and endure."

I admired his attitude and perseverance.

On April 11, 1898 Zola received a new citation that summoned him before the Versailles Assizes. The blow to the case was that only three lines of the famous letter, *J'Accuse,* were now incriminated, which narrowed the scope to make it easier for the Attorney General to try and convict his case, and make it stick this time. The trial was fixed for May 23.

On that day, crowds flocked to Versailles and the circus of irrational persecution deafened our ears. Labori, in a smart move, impeached the jurisdiction of the court on the grounds that Zola's offence had been committed in a newspaper printed and published in Paris. Hoping to ward off the enemy, he wanted to bring it back to where the majority of Zola supporters lived. To the surprise of none of us, a decision was given against him, and, once again Labori appealed to the Court of Cessation.

After a further delay and denial to change the venue, Labori stood before the Court at Versailles and raised a new demurrer. He claimed that a court-martial was not a civil person holding property and it could not sue. As with the first trial, the combative judge disallowed it.

"Then, your honor," Labori approached the bench, "I submit an application for leave to prove the whole of Zola's *J'Accuse* be accepted instead of just three lines." The reduction in size of the document the court had accepted made it near impossible for Zola to win. Without more included, not only would Zola be found guilty but nothing would be entered into the record to help exonerate Dreyfus, the main reason Zola wrote *J'Accuse* in the first place. "Your honor…"

The boisterousness in the court prevented Labori from continuing.

A pound of the gavel and "Denied!" declared the judge.

"Then," a frustrated Labori waved the transcript from the first trial, "I request that the eighteen lines allowed from the first trial be included."

The judge once more pounded his gavel to mute the commotion in the room and stated, "Quiet, or I will clear the courtroom." We held our breath for this pivotal answer and what came, not just from the judge's lips but from his entire countenance, was the same malice we had seen and heard on the streets as we rode in the protected carriage. We had been subjected to the vileness in the screams outside Zola's home before the police removed the protestors, but here in the sanctuary of the halls of justice it tightened my muscles and sickened me, the likes of which I had not felt before. "Denied," said the judge smiling the smirk of an executioner. My heart sank to the floor.

The proceedings had turned into a funeral. Three lines, a death to Zola's case, was the demise of what he had hoped for by writing *J'Accuse*. Appealing to the conscience of decent men fell on deaf ears in the court, while the opposition to rectifying a grievous wrong crushed the voices of support for justice. This was tyrannical law!

My fiery protest is simply the cry of my very soul.

Émile Zola

Chapter Twenty

It was six in the evening. The courtroom, the whole court building, and the adjoining streets were filled to capacity with people, including the anti-Semites and many army officers. They were waiting to repeat the yells of triumph bellowed at the first verdict against Zola in the Palais de Justice. Then, he had been sentenced to the maximum penalty of a year's imprisonment and a fine of three-thousand francs. Then, the corridors in the halls of justice sang out, "Death to the dirty Jews!" followed by fights that over a thousand police could hardly contain.

It was then that all bets were off and the ugliness knew no limits. Forged documents were given to the press to print that, while in the French Foreign Legion, Zola's father was a thief. It was a shock to Zola and those who knew François. Designed to discredit Zola's attempts on behalf of Dreyfus, defaming propaganda continued relentlessly. That was in May. Restless, mischievous minds were stirred up to a heightened intensity by having to wait now until July 18.

All attempts by Labori had failed, and when there was nothing to do but pursue the defense of the three lines of *J'Accuse,* he asked for a recess. The roar from the crowd muffled the sounds coming from the judge's mouth. Cold-blooded vengeance in their calloused hearts rang out as the defense attorneys whisked Zola and Perrenx away. I didn't make it to Zola's carriage in time to get past the commotion of the wild mob and the cavalry sweeping down on them that had allowed them to escape.

Starting to walk and gain a good distance, I tried to comprehend what had just happened. Heaviness like quicksand pulled at me and I sank into a morass of grief. I walked in the slow motion of disbelief and for the first time since I was a baby, I cried like one. Zola had been taken away, just like when my parents were stripped from my life. I didn't know where he'd be driven to or when I would see him again. But I knew from our conversations that were Labori to dead end as he had, he would walk out of the court with Zola and allow the judgment to go to default. When they failed to return to court the next morning, Zola would be a convicted criminal. Perrenx's attorneys would do the same.

Overactive thoughts poured forth as vacillating emotions arose from courtroom scenes turning in my head. When the trial had begun, Zola was no orator as he read his declaration with a trembling voice. But as it came to a close, he had gained composure and the courage to bear pain and danger. Where had his strength come from, when the crowd taunted, "Proof! Proof!"—which was ridiculous since the judge and military witnesses withheld proof. Knowing how difficult it was for him to speak in public, he did far better than I expected. It aggravated me to recall the way Labori had to fight for Zola, countering the grunts when he referred to him as a patriot. To this he asserted, "Yes, a patriot like Zola. A patriot with a braver heart, a clearer vision, a loftier love of his own land than is owned by any of the shallow-minded swallowers of phrases who rage at him. One of these days you will recognize your own folly and his greatness."

Wiping my eyes, I already missed my friend. The sense of his presence close by had vanished with him into the night. Trying to imagine where he was, I whispered, "Godspeed, dear man."

The past was but the cemetery of our illusions: one simply stubbed one's toes on the gravestones.

Émile Zola

Chapter Twenty-One

Wanting to lie low to avoid the wrath incurred by Zola's friends, I waited in my home for days to pass. The gray weather and weeping clouds mimicked my mood. As I gazed out my window, all I could think about was the debacle Zola's life had become. Depressing as the memories were, the sound of Labori's bellicose laughter at the Attorney General's righteous disdain made me smile. I heard Labori's voice in my head arguing the point that the Dreyfus trial had been carried out by officers whose judgment bordered on deranged and was, therefore, valueless. The anti-Semites had expressed equal irrational fervor when Labori read from Dreyfus's letters of the degradation he was experiencing in his prison cell. While the hatred spread, the pathetic communications of protest from Dreyfus to his wife Lucie formed a powerful impression of unjust devastation in the minds of those who were supportive. If only this had been entered into the record! And I abhorred that

Zola's intent for writing *J'Accuse* was for naught, for it, as well, did not make as much as a dent in the court transcript.

In need of some groceries, I waited until dusk to go out. With my head covered in a scarf and hat, I made my way past a few police who were breaking up scuffles. "Rid France of the Jewish scum," came from an elderly man moving away from a threatening cop. The irony of the argument—to protect France—was not lost on me. Guaranteed by the fundamental rights set forth in the 1789 *Declaration of the Rights of Man and of the Citizen*, a document considered by legal authorities to have equal legal standing as the French Constitution, was freedom of religion. The war of ignorance was based on enmity. *Can one even pray for intelligence? None so blind...*

§ § § §

Several very long days later I received a letter that was delivered by a trustworthy friend. My hand shook when I held it. As I opened the pages, I was relieved and grateful to see the familiar handwriting. I could hear his voice as I read that, on the last night of the trial, he was taken to a friend's home where his wife was waiting. She, his loyal companion, had remained at his side throughout the proceedings. Along with reliable friends she had clandestinely traveled to him. His mistress and the children were hidden from harm elsewhere.

"I wished we had had a goodbye hug," he apologized, "but I was whisked away too abruptly and lost sight of you. Forgive me." There was and never would be anything to pardon with my friend Zola.

We both knew that, at my age (seventy-six) and no longer possessing the energy of youth, I would not be joining him. Sorrow came from the page and my heart ached when he wrote, "I don't know when we shall see each other again." The kindness of his concern for me, with all he had to contend with, softened the ache in my body.

He went on to write that the decision to leave Paris was based on the fact that a sentence in default meant he would have to appear in person in a few days and would not be allowed to default a second time. To avoid being served, he was urged to leave France. "London was chosen as the destination." Hastily, he had made his way to the northern railway station, and took a compartment that held no other occupants.

"I made it to London without mishap and settled into the Grosvenor Hotel, which Clemenceau had recommended to me." He also mentioned that he believed Perrenx went to Belgium. Although our trust with each other had been established years ago, he still felt a need to say, "Tell nobody in the world, especially no newspaper, that I am in London. I am staying under a pseudonym. There are a few friends who followed me along with Alexandrine. It is understood by them that absolute silence of my whereabouts, to protect the most serious interests at stake, is above all in importance."

My head throbbed as I envisioned the danger he was in, were anyone to recognize his well-known face. Zola's writing and journalistic success, which afforded him the clout to publish *J'Accuse,* now worked against him. He was too famous. Many favoring the dark side of human nature would take pleasure in exposing him…if not more.

Finishing the last lines of his communication, he mentioned how the transmissions between us would happen. I held the paper close to my heart before the bright and burning flames consumed it.

Two days later, I was startled by a knock on my door. Not expecting anyone, I was relieved to encounter a cohort who had been with Zola. He said he had a message for me, but this was not the route established for written correspondence. I began to sweat. "Zola did not have time to write," he said.

Worry rang in his comment as he told me, "Counsel informed Zola that apart from English law, French authorities claimed the right to serve process on their own citizens all over the world. And," he cleared his throat, "he has been recognized."

"Oh no!"

"Fear not," he continued, "as luck would have it, it was the wife of one of his former publishers. That alone proved too dangerous for him to stay in London. He was transferred to a friend's home. That also is too close to London, so he will be seeking new arrangements as we speak."

"Then he's safe?"

"Yes," he said, "for now." Before taking leave, he assured me that Zola would get in touch with me, once settled in a secure place.

Waiting was nerve-racking as stories abounded concerning his whereabouts, which had become a main preoccupation in France. Rumors had him in Switzerland, Norway, Holland, Belgium, and other places in the world. Tensions grew when an English newspaper was onto the right track. Fortunately it came from a slip from the ex-publisher's wife who'd seen him. Cleverly disabused of that absurd idea from her husband, she was now very sorry that she had misidentified a stranger for the famous Zola.

When a small note arrived saying, "A furnished country house has been secured for me," I was comforted to know that my friend was safe. But for how long and would he ever return to his home? What is France without Zola?

To Live Out Loud

In my view you cannot claim to have seen something until you have photographed it.

Émile Zola

Chapter Twenty-Two

As the days and months moved on, Zola informed me that he was safely tucked away with house staff, writing a novel. He had been loosely planning it during the turmoil of the Dreyfus affair. For other activity, he rode a bicycle through the lush countryside north of London and took photos with a camera that was gifted to him. He wrote of the myriad scenes he had captured of farms, churches, and reaches of the Thames. Time was Zola's friend. As the cacophony in the streets condemning him to horrible fates calmed, his wife was able to return to Paris. She continued to travel back and forth to be with him, albeit under disguise.

With the shocks of anti-Semitic activity in Paris lessening, Zola's life quieted. His notes to me were filled with more trivia than concern. He spoke of his bicycle excursions and photography endeavors, difficulty with a servant getting him fish, and his need for more manuscript paper. Because leases on his residences ran out on several occasions, he was moved from home to home. Though sadly for him, Alexandrine was unable to leave Paris to keep him company because she was being watched by Zola's enemies.

Fall gave way to winter and the weeks passed. Spring 1899 brought fortuitous news. Zola, having learned enough English on his own, read with curiosity a telegram from Paris concerning Dreyfus. It stated, "Be prepared for a great success." Puzzled, as there was nothing in the newspapers, he keenly awaited further information. Soon afterwards a newspaper arrived with a story in it describing an account of the arrest and confession of the Dreyfus forger, Colonel Henry. A telegram followed stating, "Colonel Henry has been found dead in his cell." After Henry's death, Zola hoped to return to Paris. Friends, including myself, urged him to stay put. Although things had calmed in Paris, his name was still a hot iron that could rekindle the unthinkable and badly burn him. I didn't know if either of us could endure that pain again. Satisfied that the revision of the Dreyfus case was no longer a dead issue, he was content to remain in England and ride out what would inevitably be an unearthing of chaos in France.

As the review of the Dreyfus case was delayed, Zola became anxious. "Wanting to be closer to where important incidents are occurring," he wrote, referring to the fact that the

Minister of War had been replaced and Esterhazy had taken flight, "I am growing impatient."

Once again my response to him was, "Wait it out and occupy yourself with writing and your photographic cycling outings. The lapse with anything happening concerning the Dreyfus case is a storm on the horizon. Your presence might exacerbate and confuse hostilities. Let happen what will and, for the time being, stay where you are."

"You're right," he responded. "I cannot help but want to return to Paris. But for now, I shall carry her with me while I keep busy." The next letter he sent to me indicated that he'd seen in a London paper that Lt. Colonel Picquart had sent communications to the Minister of Justice concerning certain forgeries involving Dreyfus. Zola wrote, "To my mind, the report is decisive and revision is certain."

Two days later General Zurlinden, who had stubbornly opposed revision, resigned his post in the office of the Minister of War and resumed the duties of Military Governor of Paris. One of his first actions in this position was to throw Picquart in military prison. A sad letter arrived from Zola stating, "I am rather poorly today, it is one of those nervous crises that torture me."

As if this turbulent wave wasn't enough, Zola received news that his dog, a toy Pomeranian named Pinpin, which he had to leave in Paris, had taken ill. He insisted on being kept informed on his beloved pet. The dog had been Zola's constant companion. Pinpin had pined for his master since his departure after the trial. Alexandrine tried everything possible to calm the dog but it was of no use. Pinpin died. Zola, deeply attached to his little friend, was devastated. Pinpin's death threw him into bouts of angina, a chronic condition from which he suffered. When he refused to see a doctor, medicine was sent to him from France.

A friend who was there to console him relayed to me, "He broke down and cried. Then as quickly as he sank with pain, he stood straight, shook a fist and screamed, 'The scoundrels! It was they who killed him!'" referring to the anti-Dreyfusites.

The helplessness I felt over Zola's grief for little Pinpin was alleviated when I received word that the Dreyfus case had been referred to the Court of Cassation for review. I rushed a message to Zola. The news acted like an elixir, fortifying and mending him. He decided that whatever the court's decision, which he felt would be favorable, he would return to France upon the rendering of the judgment.

Not long after, on June 3, 1899, word arrived that the appeal was decided in favor of Dreyfus. He would appear before a new court-martial. Concurrent with this, the political climate was changing benevolently in the French Senate.

On the following night, Sunday, June 4, with two friends escorting him, Émile Zola returned to France. On June 5, I sat beside my tired friend as he wrote a declaration to be published in *L'Aurore*. Recalling the circumstances under which he had been obliged to leave France, he mentioned how he had been threatened and insulted and how cruelly he had suffered both before and during his exile. And, he continued, "Now, as truth has been made manifest and justice has been granted," referring to the Dreyfus case, "I return. I desire to do so as quietly as possible, in the serenity of victory, without giving any occasion for public disturbances. Even as I remained quiet abroad, so shall I resume my seat at the national hearth like a peaceful citizen who wishes to disturb none, but only desires to go on with his usual work without giving people any occasion to occupy themselves further about him."

Turning to me, he asked if I would get him a glass of wine and help myself. I gladly obliged.

Continuing to put pen to paper, Zola was peaceful when he scribed, "Moreover, my reward I have already; it is thinking of the innocent man whom I have helped to extricate from the living tomb in which he was plunged in agony for four long years. Ah! I confess that the idea of his return, the thought of seeing him free and of pressing his hands in mine, overwhelms me with extraordinary emotion, fills my eyes with happy tears!"

He took a drink from his glass of red wine, thanked me, and continued unburdening as he addressed the writing of *J'Accuse*. He went on to say he harbored no anger or resentment and that in the public interest, some example should be made of the wrong doers, for "otherwise the masses would never believe in the immensity of the crime." Then came an impassioned plea on behalf of Lt. Colonel Piquart to undo the injustice served to him. Courageously, he stated the fact that, "All former political parties have now collapsed," and that only two camps of the reactionary powers of the past remain. "Let the men who hold truth as important march toward the future."

His voice cracking, he cleared his throat. "Thenceforward, France a free country, France a dispenser of justice, the harbinger of the equitable society of the coming century, will once more find herself a sovereign among the nations. I," he sipped from his glass, "am at home. The public prosecutor may therefore signify to me, whenever he pleases, the sentence of the Versailles Assizes condemning me by default to a year in prison and a three-thousand francs fine. And we shall once more find ourselves before a jury. In provoking a prosecution, I only desired truth and justice. Today they are here. My case can now serve no useful purpose; it no longer even interests me. Justice simply has to say whether it be a crime to desire truth."

I raised my glass, silently hoping that this article, unlike Zola's first one, would be received favorably for all of our sakes.

Don't go looking at me like that because you'll wear your eyes out.

Émile Zola

Chapter Twenty-Three

Zola remained undisturbed in seclusion, while on August 8 Alfred Dreyfus was transported back to France for his new court-martial. At first hope abounded. Then a despicable assassination attempt was made on Labori, creating doubt that a positive future outcome would be achieved. Zola's silence on the matter was broken when the luckless Dreyfus was again found guilty of the crime for which he was innocent. "I am shocked by the verdict," professed Zola. Amazement at the decision spread far and wide, with the international press sharing Zola's reaction.

Newspapers around the globe contacted Zola for comment, which he declined. The astonishment on the verdict was extreme in Great Britain, and an editor of a London paper offered Zola two shillings to write what would most likely be a ten-thousand-word article. Again, he politely abstained by stating, "My dear friend, I do not take payment in France for commentary on the Dreyfus case, and still less would I accept money from a foreign newspaper."

When I inquired about why he didn't want to do interviews or write an article for the press that were asking, he told me, "For now, I have said all I want to." I never fully understood why he, who before had been so forthcoming in the press about the injustice to Dreyfus, now wanted to remain silent. I wondered if the past attempts with disastrous results had caused this reserve in him.

Shortly after the debacle of the second court-martial ended, liberal politicians brought pressure to bear on the eighth president of France, Émile Loubet. Having the facts of both court-martials, and along with the full approval of his cabinet, he offered Alfred Dreyfus a pardon. President Loubet had to weigh the protestations of the military against the possibility of throwing the country into further tumult and stirring up a civil war. This meant that he, as the executive official of the country, could set aside the punishment for a criminal act. Dreyfus was not found innocent of his supposed crimes, nor was reputation restored. This pardon, this act of clemency, only forgives the wrongdoer and restores the individual's civil rights. After this long battle with so many losses, this felt to me like a victory. I doubt if it did to those on the front lines of the fray. And what of those on the other side? Would this fan the flames of hatred once more? A shiver ran down my spine.

Five days later, and against the advice of most of his staunch supporters, bone-tired and drained after four years of solitary confinement, Alfred Dreyfus unhappily accepted the offer. He had one condition upon which he insisted: he would continue to fight to prove his innocence.

Zola's disappointment at the offering of a fig leaf, instead of a retrial and exoneration, prompted him to write a poignant letter to the poor martyr's wife, Lucie. "You have my assurance and that of my friends that we shall continue the battle until both your husband and France are fully rehabilitated."

Listening to him read his passionate words out loud to the few of us surrounding him, I was relieved to see Jacques. Knowing he was loyal to the core and was carrying a gun once again put my mind at ease. The Dreyfus pardon was by no means vindication, and even if it were, that would never have been enough to stop the escalating contempt of those roaming the streets close by. Having developed a full-fledged ulcer, I took to drinking milk. I could only imagine what was going on inside Zola's body. Although his stomach troubles resolved while in England, he suffered with angina and on multiple occasions gave me a fright when suddenly he'd grab for his chest. I wish he was as forthcoming with his personal feelings as he was with sharing his emotions concerning others and their grand-scale situations.

A constant edge crept into our daily lives as to what would become of his most recent declaration in the press. He all but urged the public prosecutor to come and serve him with papers to appear in court. As of yet that had not happened, and the dashing of hopes on the outcome for Dreyfus offered no guarantee for Zola. And so we waited.

The tenuousness of life came knocking when we received sad news that Scheurer-Kestner, who had been battling cancer, died on the same day that Dreyfus accepted the pardon. "I didn't know he was ailing," I sorrowfully responded upon hearing it.

"He was a brave man," Zola shook his head, "and it wouldn't have been his nature to bring his illness into the struggle with the Dreyfus case."

"He fought for another human being to bring light to truth while he was suffering his own ill fate." At my age, I wondered about my own destiny. I had been lucky to rise from my unfortunate beginning and live with the good nuns. And to be educated and connect with the Zolas had given me purpose. It occurred to me that it was a fortuitous thing when a man can love another, and from that relationship learn what it is to manifest the best of the human condition. I fell short of the likes of Scheurer-Kestner and Émile Zola. I am but a mere friend who has been placed by the grace of God in the best of relationships. Even with the dread of violence that Zola lives with, and by contagion spreads to us befriending him, I wouldn't trade my life with anyone.

"I have to think that his efforts in the name of truth put him to rest at peace," said Zola.

I looked at him, and with a grateful heart responded, "Yes." And wondered, what will history make of Zola?

It is not I who am strong, it is reason, it is truth.

Émile Zola

Chapter Twenty-Four

Heading into 1900, the trepidation we lived with concerning the charge against Zola of having libeled the Esterhazy court-martial still had not been addressed. In consequence of the government bringing a general Amnesty Bill before the legislature, Zola's trial had been repeatedly postponed. The tides had changed with the new government in power. We welcomed the friendlier regime. At the same time, we could not help but notice the irony when comparing Zola's treatment by the government then and now: it was like night and day. Then there was a rush to delete anything incriminating against the military and expedite Zola to a guilty verdict to appease the anti-Semitic screams and the army's hubris. Still, avoiding another debacle of injustice was in the forefront now. Also changing the political and economic climate was the fact that the World's Fair was being held in Paris. Police were already overtaxed. The government did not have the resources to waste on a divisive or sensational miscarriage of justice.

The time was favorable for an amnesty.

Zola was not in favor of (and repeatedly protested against) the Amnesty Bill. Writing letters to both the Senate and President Loubet he proclaimed, "I do not wish to be amnestied but judged." He told me he thought it despicable that the same law would be applied to him and other defenders of the truth as well as to all the wrong-doers persecuting Dreyfus.

The president had more to contend with than keeping the peace while the World's Fair was ongoing. There was also the Church: the clerical menace that had in its sights to capture France. The Dreyfus case was its weapon and under furtive direction it had gained a stronghold in dividing France. The president, with urging from his cabinet, knew it necessary to remove the fuel igniting the divisiveness. Amnesty was the answer to douse the fire. The Dreyfus Affair had to be put to rest before dealing with the Church.

In November 1900, every criminal action in the Dreyfus Affair was ceased by the Amnesty Bill, which became law. Liberties and privileges of parties were returned, while Dreyfus maintained the right to fight for revision.

Zola had lost his battle to bring the information to court and make known the wrong done to Dreyfus. The evidence was out, in the press, in conversations, and in people's minds. The facts of the case, however, hadn't been validated as truth, which was what he had hoped to achieve. Not only had he lost in court, but

Zola was also out considerable sums of money. In addition to profits from book sales, he had to sell belongings from his home to pay his bills. It is estimated that in 1897 his income was eight-thousand francs. After *J'Accuse* it was a third of that.

A personal benediction came from men helping to fight the good fight and the newspapers supporting them. Over ten-thousand francs were collected and a gold medal was made for Zola. On the heavy, sizeable medallion was his effigy. When it was originally offered to him as recognition of his courage, he refused it, saying, "The victory is not yet won."

Shortly after Dreyfus was pardoned, a ceremony was held and he consented to wear the gold medallion. A powerful speech echoing through the throngs came from Zola that day. "Undoubtedly, if the question had only been one of saving an innocent man from his torturers, of restoring Dreyfus to his wife and children, our victory would be complete. The whole world holds him to be a martyr; his legal rehabilitation will soon follow. That frightful story is surely ended! But there was another dear to us, one who was poisoned, in peril of death, and that dear and great and noble one was France. We dreamt of seeing her freed from ancient servitude, rising, with her artisans, her savants, her thinkers, to a new ideal, reconquering old Europe, not indeed by arms but by the ideas that liberate. Never had there occurred such an opportunity to give her a sound practical lesson, for we had set our hands upon the very rottenness that was eating into the cracking, decaying edifice; and we thought if we pointed it out that would be sufficient, that the house would be cleansed, rebuilt, properly and substantially. But in that respect we have been beaten. Those against us have decided merely to pass a sponge over the rottenness, so that the timbers will continue to crack and decay till the house at last comes down." In the crowd that day were Labori and Piquart.

Zola's war had been taken from him, and it took time for him to let it go. Eventually, in a calmer conscience, he settled into the comfort that he had done his duty as a man. Sympathy had come to him from all over the world (including France), yet under hushed dissents, harmful acts were talked about to shut up "the Italian" who had stained France. Along with Zola, Dreyfus was the victim of acts of violence and near misses. Replaced windows were broken, writing on the walls of their homes and screaming disturbed them in their houses, and public displays brought the police to their rescue on numerous occasions. And when a stone to Zola's head brought him to the hospital, I urged him to consider a change of residence. He refused.

Steadfast to exist without fear abusing his spirit, he went about his duties with Jacques, myself, and other friends at his side. But the Dreyfus Affair had changed him. His writing reflected that change. Zola wrote of declining faith, the delusion of hope and the travesty of charity. At the same time as he abandoned those leading principles, he replaced them with others: work, truth, and justice. Starting out believing that the individual is more important than the needs of the whole society or the group, he now adhered to a socialistic utilitarian stance. "The social edifice of men in power is more rotten than it was previously thought to be," he shared with me. The Dreyfus Affair had cemented that there was no less a call for exposure than remedial measures. He enumerated reforms, such as that every man must work for his keep, and rights should be distributed equally among citizens and not be influenced by religion. He urged that the inequity of brute force imposed from the military be balanced with civilians in the legislature, and closed doors to injustice be left opened, unless it was a matter of national security. "Should things change along this line," he smiled and continued, "then there may be a chance that another anti-Semitic debacle will not be repeated."

"That sounds very fair to me," I said.

"Yes, fair is a good word, my friend."

"Thank you."

In a spontaneous gesture, he stood and his arms surrounded me in a hug, "No, Charles, thank *you*. For all the years, through this horrible stain on France's history, there were always the friends, you at the top, who kept me sane."

Filled with warmth, "I am humbled but you didn't need to stand to do that," spilled from my mouth. I was concerned for his overexertion. Even at my age, my attention went to his body and not to the fact that I had fewer days ahead than behind me.

"Yes," his weary eyes dug deep into my soul, "I did."

Little did I know, his days ahead were even fewer…

Now look at me, I was well away dreaming like a fool and seeing visions of a nice friendly life on good terms with everybody, and off I went, up into the clouds. And when you fall back into the mud it hurts a lot. No! None of it was true, none of those things we thought we could see existed at all. All that was really there was still more misery—oh yes! as much of that as you like—and bullets into the bargain!

Émile Zola

Chapter Twenty-Five

A knock on Zola's front door startled me. "Are you expecting someone?"

"The chimney man is coming to clean it out."

A large barrel-chested man with a dark beard and greasy hair falling into his eyes entered wearing stained white coveralls. Black worn smudges were apparent on his hands, from a job I assumed he had just come from. There was something about him that made me shiver. Walking behind Zola, en route to the hearth, I caught sight of the glare he shot into Zola's back and it gave me a bad feeling. I'd seen that look on men trying to ascend into his carriage, throwing rocks through his windows, and screaming obscenities at him on the streets. My limbs grew cold as Zola, oblivious to the ill intent this man concealed, led him through his home, past Alexandrine and Jacques to where he was to work.

I rubbed the back of my neck to release the tension it held and asked Alexandrine, "Has he ever done work here? I've never seen him before."

"No, he's new," she smiled.

"How did you come upon hiring him?"

She sat up straighter and asked, "Why?"

"Just a feeling," I replied.

"I don't know how Émile found him," she said as she looked up at him approaching. "How did we hire him?" she asked.

Zola's face twitched, a nervous habit of late. "He's a poor man, hard on his luck, going door-to-door looking for work."

"He is a stranger?" I asked.

"Not any longer," Zola smiled. Then he turned serious. "What is all this fuss over a chimney sweep?"

Overthinking my reaction, I invalidated instinct, and apologized for upsetting Zola and his wife. "Just a thought," I replied.

Without querying what I had in mind, "We can certainly do with less thinking," Zola laughed, "that doesn't serve us well."

Laughter melted my anxiety and I ignored the man for the rest of the hour he was there, mostly outside. When it was time for me to leave, Jacques walked around the house to close the windows. Feeling most vulnerable while they slept, Zola and his wife shut and locked them all year round, a habit Zola regretted for he loved inhaling the fresh night air. It wasn't winter yet and the fireplace would not be needed, but when the temperature chilled, they used it to keep warm.

I reflected on Zola's supportive arrangement with Alexandrine, whom he was living with, and smiled. When it was safe to do so, he would spend time with Jeanne and the children. With every incidence of attack, his worry about his children's welfare intensified. "It was best to put space between us," he told me. "It is my love for them that requires I do this. And Alexandrine has been most generous through the years." I made my way home that night, grateful another day had been granted to all of us.

§ § § §

As days ran into months, Zola felt France was passing through the great French divide. The embarrassment had quieted and although threats were still made on Zola's life, active incidents had slowed. Feeling his work now centered elsewhere, his focus shifted to writing about capital and labor problems. He believed that the elixir for many ills was work. Influenced by the events in France, he advocated for equality and opportunity for everyone and the removal of the burdens imposed by the military and the old political force still shadowing the new regime. The movement he involved himself in dealt with comprehensive realism. Zola suggested that social conditions, heredity, and the environment all had an inevitable impact in shaping human character. My dear friend created this term—naturalism—as an outgrowth of literary realism.

The characteristics of naturalism defined Zola after the Dreyfus Affair: pessimism, and the opposite of free will, determinism. He asserted that his newly introduced fiction writing involved characters and stories based on the scientific method. Through the passing seasons, he liked to defend his new style of writing in one-sided debates, garnering supporters and eliminating some of the opposition. He laughed at the easy feat, knowing we who appreciated him were of like mind anyway.

The days of laughter became more frequent, not unlike my first months with the small child Émile and his parents. The boy had become the man, still verbose and ever brilliant. And not unlike those early days when the laughter ended, the amusement also came to an abrupt end when 62-year-old Émile Zola died of carbon monoxide poisoning, shocking everyone who knew and loved him.

Would there ever be justice for the man who gave his life in the pursuit of that very ideal.

When you have sorrow that is too great it leaves no room for any other.

Émile Zola

Chapter Twenty-Six

The circumstances surrounding the tragic death of Émile Zola were suspicious. Zola had been out with his wife for a visit to the countryside. Upon returning to their Paris home, the rainy frigid day prompted them to light a fire in their bedroom. Due to the continued death threats on Zola's life, the windows in their home remained shut while they slept. That night the coal fire emitted carbon monoxide gas which overcame them. Zola made an attempt to open the window but collapsed before reaching it.

The next morning when the servants rose and the Zolas were still in their bedroom, they knew something was clearly wrong. The door was forced open and Zola was found nearly dead on the floor with Alexandrine unconsciousness on the bed. Doctors were urgently summoned, and upon arrival they gave Zola artificial resuscitation. They were too late. He was dead. Alexandrine was taken to a clinic, and once recovered sent word for me to come. Blood drained from my head and I felt faint as she told me what had happened. She asked that I go to Jeanne and the children, Denise and Jacques, to tell them.

The shock hadn't settled in. Disbelief consumed me. The fact that he was gone was too unreal. As I relayed what had been told to me, I felt as if I was submerged under water, unable to catch my breath, living in an altered world.

Lightheaded from the news, Jeanne lost her balance and fell back screaming, "He's been murdered!" She was not the only one to suspect foul play. I did as well. Zola had made rabid enemies on the political right with his attacks on those in power over the Dreyfus Affair.

While I walked from Jeanne's home, Zola's image burned in my brain. I thought of my friend, my dearest one, who would no longer show his face and speak his words upon this earth. The ache in my chest gave way to a feeling that this might be my last day as well—death from a broken heart. The past came floating before me in slow movement and with it came the tears I could no longer contain. The street was empty but for a few stragglers; not a word about Zola was spoken for the news had not yet hit the press and public opinion. I wanted to be as far away from those who hated him for dread of what action I might take should a word be uttered against him. I made it home and tried to put food in my belly, but was instantly sick. There was no room inside me for anything but pain.

It was a mournful day when his body lay in an open coffin surrounded by flowers in his Paris house. I sat staring at the body, waiting for him to move, still in disbelief. My attention was distracted when Alfred Dreyfus entered to pay his respects and, in that moment, a strange energy moved through me, as if Zola was trying to make contact. I could almost hear the words, "The truth will come out and you shall regain your honor, Captain Dreyfus."

Dreyfus stood by the coffin, shook his head, and took several slow breaths. Turning to leave, our eyes pink from crying, made contact and I nodded a thank you to him.

Then Jeanne and the children came to the house for the first time. Solemnly quiet by the body, they stayed a good fifteen minutes before walking out, Jeanne sobbing under her breath. I was relieved that Alexandrine was still in the clinic. That she loved her husband and stood by him when he took a mistress speaks to her loyalty. It was best she was spared any embarrassment when Zola's other family arrived.

§ § § §

When Alexandrine returned from the clinic in a weakened state, despite being physically and emotionally drained, she told me, "We need to plan his funeral."

Say goodbye to Zola. Impossible. Like breathing through quicksand and speaking in a trance, arrangements were made. I don't remember those days before the funeral. October 5 was suddenly upon us. Attendance was over 50,000 at the Montmartre Cemetery, including government ministers and officials. Soldiers presented arms as the hearse passed. The juxtaposition of this respect compared with the vile attacks and cowardice during all Zola's trials exasperated me. *Where was the decency when it was most needed?* Watching the burial box make its way to the hole in the ground, I wished he could have witnessed the display of humility and dignity.

Anatole France, poet, novelist, and close friend to Zola, gave the oration. With barely a whisper from the crowd, he recalled the tribulations Zola had endured with great dignity and optimism on behalf of truth. He told what we all knew in our hearts and had seen about how Zola had lived his life. After close to thirty minutes, he said, "Zola deserves well of his country for not having lost faith in its ability to rule by law." A long pause and silence followed before he concluded with, "He was a moment in the history of human conscience."

Truth and justice, so ardently longed for! How terrible it is to see them trampled, unrecognized and ignored!

Émile Zola

Chapter Twenty-Seven

Without my friend, the heavy weight of time passed slowly. Days were lonely and painful. And as if his death wasn't bad enough, I continued to listen to the hate-filled rioting in the streets from conservative groups. They blamed the liberal changes in the political scene on the Dreyfus debacle, and Zola for his part in exposing it. Screams like, "The traitor's advocate is dead!" were too much to bear.

Visits with Alexandrine continued for many days with conversations centering on a consensual disbelief that the events that Zola was engaged in had actually led up to his death. We all feared it but, when it happened, the shock threw us into another dimension. How could humankind be so hateful and vile? As we talked, we began to process pieces of information and gossip. Riddled with guilt, I replayed the time when I read the very first article on Dreyfus's humiliation, and then later my part in supporting Zola's involvement after meeting with Lucie

Dreyfus. If I believed what my gut had told me when he was writing *J'Accuse* would I have tried to dissuade him from going forth with it? I couldn't help wondering if fear had blinded me from seeing that the worst could really happen. Jacques distracted me from my reverie when he asked, "But who would have suspected the chimney?"

"That man who came to work on the chimney." I recalled the way the chimney sweep made me feel. "If only..." I sank down in my chair.

Alexandrine interrupted with, "Charles, don't be hard on yourself. We don't know for sure if he was implicated."

Despite her kindness, I wasn't convinced. Several days later, Jacques and some other friends stopped by to commiserate. One said he had heard, "Zola's enemies had blocked the chimney, causing the poisonous fumes to build up and suffocate him."

Unable to contain the rumors that Zola had been murdered, an inquest was ordered. Tests were conducted at the Paris house. Fires were lit that showed no sign of carbon monoxide fumes, and rodents shut in the room survived without harm. The fireplace duct was dismantled but nothing of much importance was discovered, though the amount of residue found suggested that the chimney had not been adequately swept. The coroner, concerned over quieting down the situation, refused to make his expert report public and announced that Zola's death was due to natural causes.

"The coroner is doing what was done at the Dreyfus court-martial by concealing the records," a visiting friend said to me.

"Can anything be done?" I asked.

"We've been down that road before with government officials. You know the answer and," he looked at my body, "how many more years do we have?"

True, I was in my early eighties. Knowing my days were numbered, I wondered what was keeping me alive. A week later I had my answer when a surprise visitor arrived at my door. It was Lucie Dreyfus. At first I did not recognize her due to a hat and veil covering her face, I but I knew her voice the moment she spoke.

I made tea and we talked. "I know that Mr. Zola was a very important friend," she said. "You followed his every action with concerns to my husband and I thought it only appropriate to let you know that Mr. Jaures met in the Chamber of Deputies asking for a retrial of the Rennes verdict, citing the bordereau as a probable influence on the judge's actions." She went on to say, that since witness-account documentation now existed that the authenticity of the bordereau did not point to her husband, there is ground for him to be exonerated.

Jean Jaures, a French socialist leader, fought along with us for a revision of the trial. But the Marxist socialists, who did not believe in defending a man who was an officer and member of the middle class, would not approve his position. "Finally a change is occurring," I said. "This is indeed good news."

As Lucie Dreyfus's visits continued and our friendship grew, my journeying out to Zola's gravesite to share what I had learned from her decreased. Also diminishing was my energy level as my health began to decline, and soon I was confined to bed with a nurse tending to my needs while visitors came and went. More and more, I felt Zola's presence and a calm, light-filled joy entered into my home as I learned that the Criminal Chamber of the Court of Cassation had reinvestigated and ruled favorably for Dreyfus. Once that appeal was granted, the case was referred to the Supreme Court of Appeals.

As the case was on the docket, a most fortuitous event occurred changing the climate the court would rule under. The 1905 French Law on the Separation of Church and State was passed by the Chambers of Deputies. Enacted, it established state secularism, thus shifting the leadership of France to a left coalition. The power of the church-biased decisions in favor of Christianity was neutralized. It was during this momentous time that Alfred Dreyfus's case was heard by the ultimate French Court of Appeals.

My breathing was shallow when Lucie Dreyfus came to visit. With tears of joy streaming down her rosy cheeks, "It has happened," she said.

"Tell me, my dear," I labored to say the words.

Putting a hand on mine, she smiled tenderly. "The Supreme Court of Appeals, with all three chambers sitting jointly, annulled the Rennes verdict, pronouncing the rehabilitation of my husband, and proclaiming his innocence."

Moisture welled in my tired eyes, blurring the sight of her radiant face. "This is the best news." Sinking back in the pillow, I felt a deep relaxation move into my body. I watched the fuzzy vision of my friend Lucie quietly take her leave as I fell asleep.

Floating in and out of consciousness, I remember a whisper in my ear. "The Chamber of Deputies passed a law reinstating Dreyfus in the army as a major and Picquart as brigadier-general."

It is a crime to poison the minds of the meek and the humble, to stoke the passions of reactionism and intolerance, by appealing to that odious anti-Semitism that, unchecked, will destroy the freedom-loving France of the Rights of Man. It is a crime to exploit patriotism in the service of hatred, and it is, finally, a crime to ensconce the sword as the modern god, whereas all science is toiling to achieve the coming era of truth and justice.

Émile Zola

Epilogue

On July 20, 1906, Alfred Dreyfus was made Chevalier of the Legion of Honor in the same courtyard of the École Militaire where he had been degraded eleven years before. To the cheerful ovation of, "Long live Dreyfus!" he nobly responded, "No, gentlemen, no. I beg of you. Long live France!"

In 1908 Zola's remains were exhumed from the Montmartre Cemetery and taken across Paris to be interred in the Pantheon, the honored mausoleum for the great men of

France. Angry nationalists' attempts to stop the hearse were driven back by police as the coffin was placed on a catafalque.

The next day President Loubet attended the reburial. Alexandrine, Jeanne, and the two children were also present. So was Alfred Dreyfus, at whom a conservative journalist fired shots from a handgun. Dreyfus suffered a superficial wound in the arm before the police overpowered the assailant. After the commotion was over, Alexandrine, Jeanne, and the children went down into the crypt, where Émile Zola was laid to rest next to Victor Hugo and Alexandre Dumas.

To this day, the circumstances leading up to the death of Émile Zola remain a mystery.

If people can just love each other a little bit, they can be so happy.

Émile Zola

About the Author

Paulette Mahurin lives with her husband Terry and two dogs, Max and Bella, in Ventura County, California. She grew up in West Los Angeles and attended UCLA, where she received a Master's Degree in Science.

While in college, she won awards and was published for her short-story writing. One of these stories, *Something Wonderful,* was based on the real couple later presented in her fictionalized novel, *His Name Was Ben*, in 2014. Her first novel, *The Persecution of Mildred Dunlap,* made it to Amazon bestseller lists and won awards, including best historical fiction of the year 2012 in *Turning the Pages Magazine.*

Semi-retired, she continues to work part-time as a Nurse Practitioner in Ventura County. When she's not writing, she does pro-bono consultation work with women with cancer, works in the Westminster Free Clinic as a volunteer provider, volunteers as a mediator in the Ventura County Courthouse for small claims cases, and involves herself, along with her husband, in dog rescue.

Profits from her books go to help rescue dogs.

www.ingramcontent.com/pod-product-compliance
Lightning Source LLC
Chambersburg PA
CBHW060329260626
47160CB00007B/2743